REUNION

BRIAN GATTO

SEVEREDPRESS

REUNION

WWW.SEVEREDPRESS.COM

ISBN: 978-1-923165-72-4

CHAPTER ONE

They were cutting it close.

Fred Brady felt perspiration pouring down his face as if he were a window during a rainstorm. As far as he was concerned, there was no reason to live in Florida. The weather was unpredictable. Mother Nature's violent temper seemed to always hail down on the general area. Once he and his son, Joe, entered the state, it had seemed the air conditioning was blasting nonstop. At one point they were cold, and decided to turn it off, only to immediately switch the knob to on once the Florida sun beat on them through the glass.

It took a special kind of breed to make it out here. Some such were the loaders who put the cargo on the flatbed. Joe had been uneasy about this gig. Something about it being a live creature they were transporting. Fred did not pay enough mind. He saw a job and was not about to refuse the offer.

An hour into their journey, his son began fidgeting. Fred noticed and could not help himself. His son's little tick of his arm spasming from time to time was really getting annoying.

"Can you cut that out?"

"I'm just nervous."

"You've already made that abundantly clear."

Fred kept his eyes on the road but his whole aura seemed to seep into the truck cabin. Joe felt more on edge than if Fred were looking right at him. He fought to keep silent, but it was becoming harder.

Add to that the three-hour journey ahead of him and his arm was jerking around overtime.

Taking a deep breath, Fred glanced at him briefly. “It’ll be alright, kid.”

“We don’t even know what they’re having us haul! It could be some kind of shark. I hate sharks.”

“I highly doubt that.”

“How can you be sure?” Joe snapped at his father.

“Because sharks need to constantly be moving or else they drown. That tank ain’t big enough for a shark to swim around it.”

“What about a smaller shark?”

Fred chuckled. “What would Boudreaux want with a small shark? It wouldn’t be very imposing.”

“I know better than to meddle in Mr. Boudreaux’s affairs.”

The jab was intended. It cut deep despite Fred not showing signs that it did. The only thing he did do was press his foot down on the accelerator.

Deputy Jordon Wisner was growing heavy-eyed. If there was one thing he hated most about being an officer, it was patrol duty. The mundane task was almost a hobby, he was doing it so much at this point. Worst of all, there were not that many drivers on this stretch of road.

The sheriff had situated him on the least visited section of the state. It made it all the more reason to loathe the community. They had no respect for law enforcement. He wished he could bust druggies but knew his temper would land him an assault charge. It was a fact that was not lost on the sheriff. Hence why he was regulated to stopping speeding cars.

Evening was fast approaching. There would be plenty of time to lament back at home. His cow of a wife would surely bring him ham and bean stew. She had been slaving away at it all day. He would be feeling the effects of it in the morning. No doubt when he first parked in the small opening within the trees.

Jordon could name all the trees in his little nook without even looking. It was something he found comfort in. In a world of little inconveniences, the trees always listened. Not that they had much choice. To his left were a few old oak trees while his right contained bushes and vines entangled in a sea of weeds. It was no Montana, but it was enough.

He missed Montana.

The vast open space and wide view was something to admire. He had vacationed there back in '01. That was back when he dated Trudy Fawn. She was as cute as she was perky. Her attitude was always upbeat as was her physicality. Jordon wondered if he missed her or Montana more.

Why not both?

Kathy Wisner was a slouch. No one understood why he had married her. He had the keys to a goddess incarnate and he chose the chunky whale. He hated himself for it. Kathy had two things Trudy did not, and both were on her chest.

He rolled down the window and spat. "Fuckin' tits. They get ya every time."

More often than not, he found himself lamenting his life choices while amongst the trees. *Jordong the hard on* was what his fellow officers referred to him as. He was always thinking with his heart and not his head. It was the polite way of putting it.

The sky was becoming darker and his shift was almost over.

"Another waste of time." He reached forward for his keys that were in the ignition.

A beaming pair of circular lights appeared down the road. They were approaching fast. Jordon looked at them. “Figures, some hotrodder in a jeep.”

His first assumption of a jeep was quickly squashed when he realized how high up the beams were. They must belong to some truck.

“Fine, not a hotrodder. A beer belly.” Jordon chuckled as he reached forward for the siren switch. “Let’s see how he likes cherries with his diet.”

The red lights came on just as the truck passed.

“Fuck!” Fred snarled.

“Pull over,” Joe sighed.

“But… I...”

“There’s no outrunning a cop in this thing. I say we just pull over and act casual.”

Fred was taken aback by his son’s cool nature. The boy who, just minutes prior, was freaking out about being caught was now seemingly unconcerned about it all. He figured he got that mood switch trait from his mother. Although, Mrs. Brady was bipolar. He just hoped his son was not going to turn into a fruit loop in the future.

“Alright, kid. Let’s see what this pig wants.”

He pulled into a wide-open view of the swamp. The water was so clear that the bottom was visible in most spots. It was like an untouched portion of water. Not even the animals would venture here, it seemed. This was further proven when Fred rolled down his window and heard nothing. No stridulating crickets or croaking frogs. He thought it was odd but it was not on the forefront of his mind. He had priorities.

The officer pulled in behind them. He had trouble getting out of his cruiser at first because he parked in a patch of long grass. The greenery was high in the area, and he seemed to have picked the worst spot to pull them over. He eventually managed and made his way over towards the parked truck. His hat was an off-white that seemed to match his ivory skin tone. There was an all-business sense to him.

"Great," Fred sighed.

"What is it?" Joe asked.

"Looks like we got one who plays by the books."

"How can you tell?"

"How can you not? Just look at him."

Joe looked over his shoulder. He had to admit the authoritative posturing he did made him seem serious. It made him fear the officer and what could possibly happen. Perspiration began to spill down his face as if he were carrying a fever.

"Keep it cool, son," Fred stated.

Taking a deep breath, he managed to calm himself a little. "Do you think Mr. Boudreaux can get us out of this if…"

Fred hushed him. The officer was close now. Soon he was standing by the rolled down window.

"Do you know why I pulled you over?"

"Uh, yes sir. I was speeding."

"You were speeding," the officer concurred, nodding. He then looked at their trailer. The cargo container was long, longer than the cabin itself.

"Is there anything I can help you with, Officer?" Fred asked.

"Awfully big shipment you boys got there."

"Yes, and its owner is waiting. We're already late."

Officer Jordon Wisner looked back and stared at Fred. Even though his thick shades covered his eyes, Fred felt they were like daggers staring into his soul. He wanted to chuckle. The scrawny cop did not scare him. It was the possibility of him needing backup that caused him to worry.

"License and registration?" Jordon asked.

"Sure thing!" Fred fished out his wallet while Joe searched in the glovebox for the registration.

They produced both simultaneously. Jordon took them and then began back to his cruiser.

Joe let out a loud exhale.

"Don't worry, kid. We're going to be fine."

His dad forced a smile of reassurance. He did not feel like it was going well. There were going to be complications. He could just feel it in his bones.

"Remember, just this last gig. Then we can settle down somewhere."

"You've said that before."

"Mr. Boudreaux is paying us handsomely. I think it'll be well worth it this time."

"He won't pay us if we get caught," Joe added.

Jordon looked over the registration. The truck was bought in California. He wondered what they were doing all the way out here in Florida. He was curious why they were there. Especially about what was in that shipping container. He had to imply some sort of tactic or else it would eat away at him for the rest of the day.

He finished his tasks and made his way back to the truck. On his way, he looked over and knocked on the metal of the cargo.

"Hey! Are we almost done here?" Fred called out to him, obviously annoyed he was so nosey.

Reluctantly, he approached the window. "I'm going to let you off with a warning. Please be more careful."

"Will do!" Fred smiled.

Jordon turned to head back to his cruiser. The sun was starting to get to him too much. He wished he was back in Montana where the weather was more bearably cool. His train of thought was suddenly knocked off course as a loud bang came from his right. He jumped and immediately reached for his service pistol.

"What the hell are you doing? Agitating it?" Fred shouted.

"What are you transporting?" Jordon spun around.

"I don't gotta tell you nuthin'!" Fred grumbled.

"Why do you need such a big cage?"

"It likes to swim," Fred added.

"Stay right there. I'm calling this in." Jordon spun to face the truck.

"You ain't got a warrant." Fred laughed as he turned to his son. "Let's go."

He then started the truck back up.

Another loud bang could be heard and Jordon could see large sections of bulging metal starting to form.

"Holy mother of God!" the officer screamed.

A large chunk of doorway came flying off its hinges. Jordon barely had time to duck but he managed to evade it. He then recovered and got to his feet. Water was gushing out of the shipping container. There was clearly some type of tank inside. A mobile enclosure.

There was something in it.

Its head came out first. It was some kind of flat headed gator as far as he could tell. The front of its face was shaped almost like a smooth circle that arched down to a horrible mouth filled with many jagged teeth. A foot came out next. It was definitely reptilian. As the creature continued to slither out, Jordon realized there were only two front feet. It had no back feet. Its arms were two feet long at least and had sharp claws on the end.

"What is that thing?" Jordon gave a shrill cry.

"You just agitated the wrong animal, friend," Fred said as he quickly hopped out of the truck. "Get the tranquilizer gun ready."

Joe wasted no time grabbing the box, retrieving the weapon and loading a dart into the chamber.

Meanwhile, Fred watched as the officer began to back away. "I wouldn't do that if I were you. Could agitate it."

Jordon began to fumble, grabbing his pistol. He finally managed to unclip it just as the monstrosity crawled the rest of the way out of the tank. He quickly raised his weapon and took a deep breath, lining up his shot.

A dart, the size of a sewing needle with some pink fur on the end, struck him in the stomach right above the groin. He immediately began to feel its effects as he stumbled backwards. He tripped over himself and landed on his rear.

"Load it up again! We need it back!" Fred ordered his son who looked pale.

"I didn't mean to hit him," he said.

"What's done is done. Load the gun!"

The creature wasted no time at all crawling towards the barely lucid man. He wore a terrified expression that was soon replaced with one of agony. He could barely find the strength to scream as the reptilian beast bit down onto his leg. It tugged hard enough that Jordon could hear his muscles popping and feel tendons pulling. A juicy ripping sound came as it bent his leg in an awkward direction and then pulled. It came off like a chicken leg being torn from the bird's body. Blood shot out as it pumped through his system, making for one continuous spray.

"Shoot it!" Fred cried.

Joe tried to line up his shot, but the creature was moving too fast now. It had tossed the leg and went for the more bountiful contents. Chomping down on his crotch, its teeth were just around his abdomen. It bit down hard and then gave a mighty pull. As his privates were ripped from him, so too was a portion of his stomach. The officer's innards spilled out onto the bright green grass as the creature swallowed its morsal. Then, it slurped up his guts like noodles. It made Joe feel ill.

Before Fred could command his son to sedate the creature again, it bit down on the lawman's midsection and made a beeline for the swamp.

"It's getting away!" Fred screamed in a shrill voice.

It dragged itself into the swamp, slipping beneath the surface. The last thing either man saw of it was its spiked tail disappearing below. As water passed by its scaly body, it felt a sense of familiarity. The swamp was now its domain. Its territory. Its home.

"What have we done!" Fred said coldly. He quickly took the cap off his head and brushed the top of his bald head. His sideburns were drenched in sweat as was his beard. He had gone from looking comfortable to a total wreck in a heartbeat.

"We have to contact Mr. Boudreaux," Joe said.

"I know," his father sighed. "It's not a call I'm looking forward to. At all."

Just then, a phone rang. Fred was about to pick his up to perform the task when he heard it.

He flipped his open. "Hello?"

There was no one on the other end.

"It's coming from over there!" Joe pointed towards the police cruiser.

His son hurried over and retrieved the cellular device.

"Don't answer it, boy!"

The name Kathy Wisner read on the screen with a picture of an obese woman petting a cat situated centered above.

"I think it's a woman."

Fred approached and took the phone from him. He saw the picture. “Probably just some cat lady calling about a missing pet.”

“On his personal phone?”

His father sighed. “Shit. Probably the poor sap’s wife.”

“What now?”

“Now? Now I call Mr. Boudreaux, and we figure out this thing.”

“I mean about his wife.”

Without thinking, Fred tossed the phone out into the swamp. “We didn’t see anything.”

Joe gulped.

“It’s better this way. We either do our job or go to jail.”

“We didn’t kill that cop!”

“No.” Fred looked out into the swamp. “More people will die if we don’t stop what did though.”

CHAPTER TWO

It was not possible.

There was no way it could have been ten years already. It seemed too high a number. Mark Stanton saw it as outlandish to even suggest it had been a decade since he graduated high school. Had time truly flown by that fast? It had to be a joke, some asinine prank sent by a sorry sack of lard. It was not though. He read the notification on his phone. The number was from the Wyman High School of Florida State.

Mark slouched on his vintage recliner from the 1970s. It had been a gift from his uncle before he passed. The furniture piece stuck out like the odd duck in his living room, but he refused to part with it. As he sat in the old musky, stained seat, he read the message again. It seemed clean and professional, something that would be written by a secretary and sent out in a group text or email. It was real, he had accepted that much.

It began to weigh him down. He felt cold and alone. Save for his dog, Buster, he was in isolation. The cabin he resided in was off a beaten path with no internet connection and barely any service. His parents thought he would have achieved more in his life but were supportive of whatever he chose to do. Which was not much.

His work ethic was flexible. He had unlimited time and found work at odd jobs here and there. Besides his dog, who was turning eight this summer, he had the occasional woman over. That was one thing he carried from high school. It was not his confidence or communication. He was as handsome as the star football player just without muscles or girth.

Placing the phone on his lap, old Buster came waddling over with his three legs. The dog had a knack for telling when something was off with his owner.

"It's alright, boy." He gave the dog a pet.

Buster looked at him with sullen eyes. He was a skinny dog. Food was not cheap, but he fed him as much as he could. The labrador was over friendly and Mark's female guests found him irresistible. Most of them at least. There was one cat person he met who drove him crazy. She could not leave his house soon enough.

"I guess I'll have to leave you with Barbra in a couple of nights."

The animal's ears perked up at the mention of the elderly neighbor with the wrinkly hands and pocket full of goodies.

Mark hated taking advantage of the older woman, but she never minded. He chuckled as Buster let out a low growl followed by a loud bark.

"I take it you won't miss me very much."

His tail wagged.

"Then that settles it! I'm going to my class reunion!"

***

Paradise was an understatement to Tina Bessy. Kaui Hawaii was more a tropical heaven. Everyone was friendly, the ocean was tranquil, and the weather was not overbearingly hot. It was a far cry from her birth home in Florida where she grew up and went to school. She had no real interest in ever returning there.

If anyone had asked when she graduated, she would have had no idea. She barely remembered most of her fellow students, let alone her teachers. It was not a personal choice. She always knew her personality was too big for Wyman High. Boys called her too bubbly, other girls poked fun at her abnormally large breasts. She was proud of her body and how well she had taken care of it now. Back then it was a different story. She hated herself.

Only one boy seemed to enjoy her company. He was not flirtatious. Instead, he stood up for her when others beat her down.

When she got the text about the reunion, she smiled at the group of people who would be attending. Namely Mark Stanton. He had written *See you there, class of 2015*. There was a smile emoji at the end of it. She chuckled at that.

"Let's go, Ms. Bessy!" A photographer that she had already forgotten the name of, ushered her over by the pool side.

"Where's Carlos?" she asked.

"He's over by the trailer."

She looked over and saw her manager on the phone, presumably talking about her upcoming shoot in California. She was not looking forward to it. She had been there before. The place was not as lively or safe as it used to be.

"I'll be right back," Tina told the photographer.

She did not wait for him to answer. Instead, she hurried over to Carlos and put on her best smile. He did not seem impressed.

"What is it now, Tessy?"

"It's Tina," she corrected him. "I have an event I want to attend. I need to leave on the first flight to Florida."

"No can do, kiddo."

"What?"

"We have that shoot in California coming up. I can't have you across the US for some event. Besides, you'd have to take at least three flights to get there.

Honolulu Airport is a two-hour drive from here," Carlos explained.

She looked down at herself regretfully. Here she was, dressed in a beautiful green metallic two-piece that fit her comfortably and she had no one to impress.

"Don't look so down, kiddo."

"I need to get there. Can we call Burt over at his studio, see if he minds rescheduling?"

"It's too late. I'll be charged a fee."

"Please, Carlos. I never ask for anything."

Carlos looked at her. He usually never felt pity for his models, but Tina was different. She was a sweet woman who just happened to be drop dead gorgeous. He then looked around over at his other models.

"What're you thinking?" she inquired.

"I'm looking for another red head to replace you."

"What about Tanya? She is not as buxom but she'll pass."

"Who's Tanya?" Carlos asked.

"You really need to get better at remembering names," Tina chuckled and then pointed over by a bus. "She's in trailer three."

"You owe me," Carlos told her.

"I sure will!" Tina quickly made her way over towards the estate.

The photographer approached Carlos. "Where the hell is she going?"

"Florida."

"I don't do Florida," he replied.

"That's alright. I've got something for you to do," Carlos said as he walked him over towards Tanya's trailer.

Tina, meanwhile, began to pack her bags feverishly. She placed a shirt and pair of jeans over her bikini outfit. There was no way she was leaving without it. She hurried to her car and waved Carlos goodbye. He gave a half-hearted smile.

Once she hopped in, she grabbed her phone and pulled open the group chat. "See you there!" she said as she wrote.

She then ended her sentence with a wink emoji.

***

As far as Leon Tate was concerned, if anyone could convince him to miss an afternoon of gym session to go to some class reunion, it was George Barkley. The man was a beginner in the art of lifting weights but had the determination and drive to achieve greatness. Both men would not compete against each other but rather worked together, to better their strengths.

Leon may not have been aware, but he meant the world to George. If it were not for him, George would have been desperately trying to figure things out on his own.

George pushed up a hundred-pound barbell while Leon spotted him.

"You got this!"

The encouragement reinvigorated his drive, and he managed to get it set back on the hooks while Leon stepped back and clapped his hands together.

"That's what I'm talking about, man!"

George let out an exhale and then sat up. "So, you'll come?"

"I'm not sure." Leon turned towards the dumbbell rack.

"C'mon, bro. You said if I got fifteen reps with a hundred pounder that you'd agree."

Leon nodded. "Your girlfriend sure plans shit last minute."

"Yeah, well. I've gotten used to just going with the wind."

"Okay," Leon chuckled.

"I'm serious. I never knew how much of a stress relief it would be to not plan everything so intensely."

"Just wait until you get that new job as a teacher. I'm sure they'll love to hear about your stress relief."

"Don't harsh the moment, man," George laughed. "Are you coming or not?"

Both men stood there silently. Leon lifted a dumbbell, sat down and proceeded to do some curls. "Who else was on the list?"

"She won't tell me. Apparently, she sent out a group text but excluded my number and yours."

"What's the catch?" Leon asked.

"I assume she wants it to be a nice surprise."

"Or a trap."

"Zoe's not like that," George told him.

"No offence, man, but you and Zoey are not getting along that well. Are you sure she isn't up to something?"

"Like I said, she's not like that."

Placing the dumbbell on the floor, Leon looked up at his friend. "This better be worth it man." George held out his hand and they fist pumped. "Don't worry. You won't regret it!"

"I better not. First sign of trouble and I'm out."

"I won't stop you," George laughed.

They did not leave the gym until late morning. It had been a rigorous work out for both of them, but Leon was feeling the burn and loving it while George was exasperated and needed a cool beverage. They entered the parking lot and noticed a juice vendor cart opening.

"Want to get a drink?" George asked.

"It's too early."

He laughed at the response. "Juice. I was talking about juice, man."

"Where?" Leon wondered as he peered around the area.

"Looks like a stand is open for business. Let's check it out."

Leon nodded as they walked over. There was a beautiful African American woman manning the cart. She had a pixie hair cut and a dazzling smile which she welcomed them with.

"What can I help you boys with?" She paused. "Wait, aren't you Leon Tate?"

"The one and only." He grinned. "I have my own column in the town paper about fitness. You a fan?"

"I've read it but that's not where I know you from." She seemed giddy.

They both took a moment to look over her face. She was beautiful but both men could not figure out where they recognized her from. They shrugged.

"I'm Cecilia. Cecilia Dower!"

George was still a bit hazy on who she was, but Leon's heart skipped a beat. "No way!"

She noticed George was still confused. "I used to have braces and pigtails back in high school." "I'll be damned." Geroge suddenly remembered. "How've you been?"

"Oh, you know. Just running my little Jolly Juice stand here."

"Wasn't that your mother's job?" George wondered.

Leon wanted to jab him with his shoulder but fought the urge. She noticed he seemed annoyed.

"It's alright. My mom retired two years ago. She needed a break."

"Rightfully deserved!" Leon smiled.

Cecilia blushed.

"What year did you graduate?" George asked her.

"2015," she answered. "I was a little younger than you guys but still a senior."

"It's been a long time," Leon beamed.

"Yeah, ten years to be almost precise," George continued. "We are having a class reunion in two days. Do you think you could get an afternoon off from work?"

Leon looked over and almost wanted to hug him. He did not think George would even have the gall to ask anyone. He figured he would let Zoey do all the work in finding fellow classmates.

Cecilia smirked. "I think I could spare a few hours."

"Great! We'll meet you down by the marina at, oh say one o' clock?"

"The marina?"

"Yeah. It's a boat trip. We're going to ride all the way to the school."

"How many others are going?" Cecilia inquired.

"Me and Leon, and my girlfriend Zoey who sent out a group text to everyone. I'm not sure how many but there'll be at least four of us."

Cecilia looked from George to Leon. She seemed nervous.

"Is that okay?" George asked.

"Well," her voice trailed off.

"I promise, it'll be a clean boat trip. No booze besides some champagne," Leon said.

"Plus, the trip is only for an hour or so. We'll be back in town before five," George added.

She did not seem convinced yet.

"Is there anything we can do to make it more comfortable for you?" Leon asked sincerely.

Cecilia let out a sudden bellow of laughter. "Oh guys. You're so sweet! I'll tell you what. Lift the booze ban and I'll bring some special juice."

Both men erupted into laughter.

"You've got it, sista!" Leon said.

"Oh, and one more thing," Cecilia asked.

"What's that?" George whipped a single tear from his eye.

"Should I bring a bikini? I mean, if we're going to be on a boat."

"No objections here!" Leon clapped his hands together.

"Okay! Sounds good! I'll see you!"

George and Leon turned to leave and saw a small line forming behind them. Leon was happy she was doing business. If she had just opened and there was already a crowd forming, there must be something to her beverages after all.

***

Zoey Francis sat at the edge of her bed looking over her pad of paper. With a pen tucked carefully behind her ear, and plenty of empty pages to go through, she began jotting down names. So far, Mark and Tina had accepted. There were several other people who were attending the reunion but none of them seemed to want to go on a boat.

The door shut downstairs, and she heard the heavy footsteps of George making his way to their bedroom. He opened the door and walked across the wooden floor towards their bathroom.

She did not smile, nor did she greet him. Instead, she focused on her paper. He did not seem to notice. The water turned on from the overhead faucet and he began to hum a tune in a bland tone.

Though it was not his fault, she could not stand his voice. She tried to focus on her paper. Going as far as covering an ear with her shoulder, it did no good. The humming seemed to die down as did the water. She heard the swoosh of the curtain opening and was momentarily relieved that the humming stopped. The brief reprieve would not last long.

After a couple of minutes, he walked out of the bathroom and over to his dresser. He pulled out a pair of underwear and put them on. "Anyone agree to come along?"

"A couple."

"Oh? Well, me and Leon got Cecilia to come."

"Who?" she wondered.

"Remember? Dower the frowner?"

"Why'd you invite her? I thought you couldn't stand her."

"Leon seemed interested. She looks a lot better without those braces and pigtails."

"I see."

George made his way over and peered over her shoulder. There were two names in her notebook. The top was Tina. His interest was piqued until he saw the next name.

"You didn't!"

"It's a reunion. I couldn't not invite him!"

"That low-life scum is going to show up and ruin the party! What were you thinking?"

"You guys used to be friends."

"Yeah, and if I remember correctly, you both were a little more than that."

"That was before *us*."

"Ha!" George walked around to stand in front of her. "Tell him not to come."

"I can't. He and Tina already agreed to come along. Besides, I think Tina likes him. Maybe it won't be so bad. Maybe…"

The slap took her off-guard. She had been expecting it all morning. Ever since Mark sent the reply he agreed to join in. Still, it did not make it any less painful.

"You think this is a game?" George wanted to hit her again but realized she might bruise. He did not want to have to explain to everyone at the reunion why she was covered in layers of make-up.

"I think..."

"No!" he cut her off. "You don't get to think. You get to do as you're told. I'm telling you to uninvite him."

She reached up and held her cheek. "You have a phone. I'll give you his number."

It took every ounce of restraint to not slap her again. "Watch your tone!"

He then stormed over to his dresser, finished getting his clothes on, and made his way downstairs. She heard him rummaging through the fridge, looking for leftovers. She was thankful it was not beer he desired. Although, he had become more violent since he stopped drinking so much.

Maybe I should run down to the store and get him a six pack. Let him kill himself. I don't care anymore!

Instead, she lay on her back and wondered about the next two days. She hoped more people would agree to come. If not, George would think it was a waste of time and money and probably get violent again.

CHAPTER THREE

Caution overruled impulse.

Fred Brady had been contemplating calling his employer for thirty-six hours. His son had urged him to do so. Human lives were at stake, he knew that his son knew that. No one else did. It was not up for discussion as far as Joe was concerned. Still, Fred evaded his son's persistent nagging about morality.

They had pulled into a motel parking lot shortly after the incident with the cop. Joe was continuously pacing back and forth in their rented room. The light cast by the sun through the window was blocked by his movements, creating an erratic shadow. One that passed by Fred as he tried to rest.

"I don't know how you can just sit there!" Joe said suddenly.

"I don't know why not. As far as I'm concerned, that creature has its new home."

"I didn't know you advocated for animal relocation."

"I don't," Fred muttered.

"You sure seem like you do, acting all smug and content while that thing's slithering around out there!"

"I chose to shake it off. There's no way Boudreaux can pay me enough to go toe to toe with that thing."

"Great!" Joe stormed towards the door. "While you ignore the problem, I'm going to get a drink."

Fred did not argue as his son walked out. The boy was losing his edge. In that, he was becoming weaker. After a few minutes, he stood up and made his way over towards the window. He looked out and saw him chatting up some dark woman behind a juice stand.

His phone suddenly rang. He reached into his pocket. He looked down his side and saw the caller ID. *Boss Man.*

"Shit," he grumbled.

It rang on and on. He was about to put it back into his pocket when his finger accidentally hit the button to accept the call. He reluctantly raised the phone to his ear and spoke into it.

"Hello."

Fred had half expected to hear shouting or, at the very least, a stern voice. Instead, the tone was more joyous.

"Mr. Brady! How are you?"

"I'm fine, Mr. Boudreaux."

"I heard about your little accident."

"Oh?"

"Yes. Terrible news about the cop. Even worse, my product escaped into the swamp. I can't fathom how many people are in danger now."

Fred wanted to laugh. He knew his employer did not care about human life. The only repercussions he feared were financial and his own reputation. He fought the urge. "Yes. About that. What exactly was it we were transporting?"

"A surprise." He heard a low, maniacal giggle on the other end.

"For who?"

"For whomever I please." Fred could practically see Mr. Boudreaux grinning insidiously on the other end with his wide smile and yellow-stained teeth.

"I think the more details you share the better. If you want me to get it back, I'm going to need to know everything about it."

"Who said I wanted to hire you two again? If I want it back, I'll need professionals."

"You know me, Mr. Boudreaux. I can track shit through mud."

"That's besides the point. You already screwed me once before. Either you are not loyal, or you are a bad investment."

"Hey. C'mon, Mr. Boudreaux. I think it's clear what's going on here. We were ill-prepared, it escaped. What, are you trying to have it go on a test run? See how it does in the wild?"

There was no response.

"I think if you want it back, you'll hire us. We're the closest to its location. If we get the information we need, we can recapture it easy peasy."

Fred could tell his employer was deep in thought. He did not respond for seconds but that gap in time told him everything. "We're doubling our fee."

"Fine, twenty thousand."

"Plus, an extra five thousand for secrecy."

"Deal," Fred said.

"You really need to learn what you're worth, Mr. Brady. I'm hiring you cheap compared to what I'd pay another hunting party."

Before Fred could answer, Boudreaux cut him off. "Here is what you're dealing with."

Joe had not kept track of the time while he was out in the plaza. He had walked by several shops, a gym, and the juice stand with the lovely server. He decided to head back when the skies turned a shade of red that was both beautiful and ominous. He knew it was usually a good sign of nice weather, but he could only be reminded of blood. The sight of the cop being torn apart like that made him shiver. He wanted to reach down and feel if his manhood was still intact but reminded himself, he was in public.

As he used the spare key to unlock the door, he heard some harp music playing behind it. *He can't seriously be listening to some classical shit right now, can he?*

He walked inside and saw his father sitting in front of an old bulb television. It was out of date and the picture quality was about on a par with the quality of film that he was watching. There was some buxom blonde swimming along the surface. She was suddenly interrupted during her butterfly stroke by a minisub appearing seemingly out of nowhere. A man was inside, and he opened the hatch and tried to start a conversation with the woman.

Much like her, he showed no interest. The film was in black and white, and he always grew tired and bored of those.

"What's the news?" he asked his father.

"Well, this isn't CNN or FOX. This is a movie."

"I mean with the cargo,." Joe said, annoyed.

Fred sat up from the bed and inched closer to the television. "You know he died recently. He had a good run. A damn good run. He was an important figure in the world of B-grade cinema."

"Who? That guy?" Joe looked to the television briefly.

"No. The director. Although he mostly produced films. Did you know that one of his biggest successes was a film about a half shark and half octopus."

"Fascinating," Joe feigned interest. "What's that got to do with the gig?"

"Because, son," Fred reached forward and turned the knob until the television went dark. "We're going hybrid hunting."

***

Neil Raymond was growing impatient. He used to love his line of work, taking tourists out to fun and exotic locations in the swamps of Florida. Lately, the whole business was draining his enthusiasm. He was sick and tired of complaints. They were usually about things out of his control. He got several three stars because it rained.

There was no doubt the money was tight, and he had bills to pay. He had to make ends meet where he could. Several nights last week he had to settle on ramen for dinner. The only star amongst his cloudy life was that the harassment reviews that were on his charter's webpage had been removed. He was good, for now.

Now, standing before him, was the picture-perfect horny couple. The man continuously grabbed his girlfriend's rear and squeezed, causing her to jump and playfully slap his hand away. Neil had to admit she was a looker. She wore big golden hoop earrings and had shoulder length, wavy reddish-brown hair. She was clearly European, the kind of woman he rarely got to see outside of film and magazines.

Her boyfriend was a muscularly built individual with more biceps than brains. He had been explaining to him all morning that his boat was rented out for the afternoon but the numskull wouldn't have it.

"Do you have a rowboat or something? I want to take my girl here out for a pleasure ride."

I'm sure you do, Neil inwardly chuckled.

"It's no big deal," his girlfriend said. "We can just walk on the grass near the river."

"Screw that! I want the full experience."

"Trent, let's just go."

Of course, the guy's name is Trent, Neil thought as he raised his hands up in surrender.

"Listen, there's no big boat for hire. I do have a rowboat."

"A rowboat?" The woman's eyebrow arched.

"C'mon, Ava. Let's try it!" Trent asked her.

Ava thought long and hard. She had promised him something out of the norm. A wild ride. A new environment. She just did not want to be eaten alive by bugs.

"Do you sell bug spray?"

"The best in town." Neil smirked and reached under the counter.

He fished out a large can of a chemical called *Bug Be Gone*. "It'll kill any insect."

"Is it hazardous to my skin?" she asked, briefly rubbing her tanned arm.

"I use it all the time. It never hurt or damaged me. I also know what's in it."

"Oh yeah?" Trent asked.

"Yep. Secret recipe."

"You made that shit?" Trent laughed.

"Kind of. My dad taught me the perfect concoction and here it is."

"Does it smell?" Ava inquired.

"Like flowers."

"Well, at least it's not piss and mud," Trent laughed. "How much for it and the boat?"

"Five for the can, forty for the boat."

Trent reached into his back pocket, took out his wallet, and produced a fifty. "Keep the change."

"Much obliged." Trent tucked the money into the register. He then turned around and took a key off the wall. "It's down by the dock, the third slick."

Handing Trent the key, he tightened his grip. "Take care of her."

"Don't worry." Trent gave a sideways glance to Ava. "I will."

"I'm talking about the boat."

Trent chuckled and slung an arm around Ava. The two then walked out of the building.

Neil took a seat in his leather chair and began looking through a fishing catalogue. He wished he was in Montana or Tennessee. Florida was nice, just too hot all the time.

***

The environment was familiar. As the serpentine creature slithered around, it sensed certain spots that struck a chord, a memory. Patches of bright green grass felt good against its scaly hide. Sections of mud and water were abundant. The whole area was coated with unpredictable environmental locations like that. One spot could be hard ground while the next was wet and smelly.

It traveled at a slower speed than normal. Its massive head was weighing it down a bit. With the massive cranium, most of its senses like smell and vision were heightened. Reaching out with these attributed gifts it had been bestowed, it inhaled the scent of prey. Taking a huge whiff, the pungent odor was not familiar to it. Yet it was irresistible.

Picking up the pace, it soon came to a smaller creature. It had long legs and a pair of growths sticking out of its head. As soon as it spotted the inferior animal, it too turned tail and ran. There was sport now, a chase. It was hopping across pits and bumps of grass, making good haste.

The hunter was faster though.

Before it even had a chance to slow, the slithering serpentine hovered over it, keeping pace while gaining slowly.

Suddenly, it lunged forward and snatched the mammal in its powerful jaws. It bit down, hard, snapping one of the legs in an awkward direction in the process. It swallowed its prey. The taste of blood coated its tongue like a drip of adrenaline. It invigorated the specimen as if it were a kid letting some liquid candy spill down into their mouth. It was satiated for the time being and slowly crept towards the water's edge. Soon, the water grew deeper. It sank to the bottom and rested.

Other critters approached but none dared to go too close. It opened its jaws, almost beckoning them to do so. The only ones brave enough to venture lacked any real instincts besides feeding. They were small fish and some mollusks and clams. They swam around the cavernous orifice. The creature did not attack as they pecked at its gums, effectively cleaning out its teeth.

The mighty king of the swamp.

CHAPTER FOUR

It was clear.

To George Barkley, the obvious thing was to play along. The whole idea was ludicrous though. To attend a high school reunion was one thing. To assemble one for Wyman was another. The school did not have the best track record for successful students. Some were gifted; most were white trash. The ratio of decent turnouts to meth addicts was practically tilted. The former was way down on the lower end.

Zoey had other motives. George suspected that. In his mind he knew it was true. She had begun to grow bold the last couple of years. Sneaking out to hang out with friends was one thing but to come back home slung around a man's shoulder was another. He had claimed he was just helping her get home and that he owned the bar down the street. George had him leave with a black eye and a restraining order. That meant being banned from the local establishment as well. It was something he held over his woman's head like a raincloud.

No, he thought. *I'll figure out what the deal is. She has Mark on board. Perhaps he was in on her little escape plan. Fuckin' guy. Women only liked him because of his long shlong.* It was a fact he would never admit to. He caught a glimpse of the appendage sophomore year after gym class. He doubted even Leon would buy that story.

His mind continued to wander as he stared at the television. There was a report of a missing officer, but it did not register in his cloudy thoughts. He only snapped out of it when he saw Zoey making her way past the window and towards the front door.

She opened it and stared.

"You're five minutes late," George stated.

"Long line at the market."

"Mmhmm." He placed the empty beer bottle he had had a firm grip on down on the table in front of him.

She scoffed, "Please put it on a coaster."

George did not pay her any mind. "How many are coming now?"

"It's still the six of us. Everyone else is going to be on the other side of the lake near the school."

"Why are we doing this?" George reached forward and absentmindedly reached for a coaster.

"I just want to catch up with everyone."

"Why go out on a boat then? We could just as easily drive out to the school."

Zoey took a deep breath. "Originally I wanted to but I owe the boat guy."

"What?" George's tone changed from mild to tempered instantaneously.

"Relax. He gave my car a jumpstart when it broke down in front of his shop last summer. Remember, I told you that."

"So he wants you to, what? Rent a boat?"

"He's had a couple of bad seasons. I figured it would be a nice favor."

"I know Neil. Kind of. Anyway, he hates young people. Why would he even consider helping you out when you could've called the shop? Furthermore, why would he want you to rent out a boat?"

"Desperate people do desperate things." Zoey shrugged as she brought her groceries into the kitchen.

George stood up and followed her. She was bent over, moving stuff around the fridge. There were several beer cans and plates of old food that she was destined to toss out after she was done putting the food away.

"I think we need to discuss Mark coming."

"You and Leon had no problem inviting Cecilia."

"Out of the kindness of our hearts."

"Don't bullshit me! I saw her at the market. She approached me. I didn't even recognize her at first. She was excited about the reunion. I can't believe she's still in this shithole town and not out modeling in California or something."

He gulped. "I, uh..."

"What? Were you not going to tell me? Maybe wait until we got there and I found out."

"She's all Leon's. I swear."

"Yeah. Sure. The African King and Queen of the swamp. They'd make a great pair as long as it's consensual."

"You're being a bit racist, honey."

Zoey took another deep breath. "I'm being observant."

He watched her as she dug out the food from the plastic bags. "You can be observant all you want. Doesn't change the fact that you're trying to run away from me."

She chuckled, "Don't tempt me."

"I'm losing my patience."

"What patience? Was it patience that gave me a black eye last week?"

"Look, I'm sorry. I can't control myself sometimes. I just get so angry."

The refrigerator door slammed. She spun around and got close to his face. "Why are you always so angry, huh?"

"Because. You don't appreciate me."

“It wasn’t my first injury!”

“It won’t be your last unless you learn to listen!”

Zoey’s eyes began to water. “I don’t deserve this.”

“Oh, here we go again. Woe, is me!”

“You’re a goddamned hypocrite!” She turned back towards the unit.

“I am not!” He raised his hands forward and shoved her.

She was sent stumbling forward, nearly banging her head against the handle. Reacting quickly, her hand shot forward and she caught herself on the door.

George looked baffled. “I’m sorry, babe!”

There was no response. She turned and walked out of the room. “Put the rest of the groceries away!”

“We’ll have to take them all back out today anyway,” George whined.

She did not answer. Eventually, he left the kitchen and sat back down on the ratty couch. He reached for the remote and turned the television off.

***

There were several stops from Hawaii to Florida. Tina was thankful everyone was patient, and that jetlag did not wear her down. She was excited to see old, familiar faces. Namely Mark Stanton. The very thought of him drove shivers down her back. She wanted to see how much everyone had changed. Most of all, if Mark was still as dashing as he had been before.

Landing in Florida and exiting the plane, she was overcome with the humid climate of the region. She had been mentally prepared for it. It was like an old friend. A really hot old friend. Most of the passengers were already fanning themselves and sweating profusely. She was the only one who was able to enjoy the wretched weather.

Making her way down the boardwalk, she hailed a cab. There was no problem there. While most of the tourists were practically shouting at the drivers to pick them up, she had gotten first dibs on one. The pair of dark eyes watched her. They tried to regard her cooly but there was a sense of desperation.

She just hoped he would be civil and not some slobbish pig.

When she opened the door, the latter had come true. The back was cluttered with empty bottles and fast-food wrappers. There was no obscene odor. She peered inside and saw why. Hanging from the rearview mirror were several air fresheners in the shape of trees. There were more than five. Seven or eight maybe.

"Need any help?" he asked.

"I'm fine." She went to shut the door.

"You need a ride?"

"Yes, but…"

"Then let's get you to where you need to go," he said, cheerfully.

She gave a faint smile. Her look of dissatisfaction was apparent. Still, she did not want to be rude and set her bag down. She then scooted inside.

"Where to?"

"Um, Raymond's Rides? At least, I think that's the name of it." She gave an unsure grin.

"Ah, yes. Neil's place. Alright. I'll take you there. Shouldn't take more than twenty minutes."

"Great," she said and then shut the door.

The cab took off. As they made their way down a road, she took in the familiar sights. A lot hadn't really changed in ten years. Some of the shops and houses were still the same. She saw Mr. Beardsley's estate, an old Victorian-style home. It was beyond a set of wrought iron gates but was still visible to the public. The rumor was he had inherited the property from his late sister. He was a teacher at Wyman. His career was not filled with prosperous fortune. In fact, it was a rather low-end job. Certainly not a position one could afford such a luxurious home with.

She then passed several plantations. The wide-open farmland was overgrown with cotton and shrubbery. The descendants of the ancestors that once owned them had either sold, moved on, or neglected the area some time ago. The general public did not blame them. The history of those homes was problematic in modern society.

Soon, they were in the swampier sections of the town. It was not the everglades, but it was a thriving habitat nevertheless. Tina had often wondered why a school was built so close to it. She had heard the owner of the property donated it but that had to have been over fifty years ago. The school was not new. In fact, it was in desperate need of repair.

If one were so inclined to bestow a public school near a swamp, it would also be expected to not be placed anywhere near the water's edge. From the front doors to shoreline was approximately a football field's distance away. When it rained, the basement of the school was flooded. Sometimes it would even seep to the first floor. It was a wonder the school had not been closed down years ago.

The cab driver continued on. He had been rather silent the whole trip. There were casual glances in the rearview mirror. She pretended not to notice.

Eventually, the bayou turned into a babbling brook. There were several dry sections of the swamp where one could trek and hunt through. There was a way around it by boat but most just hoofed it or called it quits at the inlet. As they went further the waterway opened up more. It revealed a large creek. The open body of water stretched for miles. The grassy path turned into a road. She had not noticed how much of it had been overgrown until the ride became smoother.

Raymond's Rides was just up ahead. There were four vehicles in the parking lot. One was clearly Neil Raymond's. Not only did it have fishing gear in the bed of the truck but the business logo had been plastered on the doors.

A big SUV was parked close to the entrance. It was practically nudging Neil's truck. As the taxi approached, it backed up suddenly. The cab driver slammed down on the brakes and began cursing under his breath. The SUV had stopped and he shouted for them to move as if the driver could hear him.

"Sorry, miss."

"It's alright," Tina said.

Eventually, the vehicle was reparked. This time, it was further from Neil's truck. The cab driver pulled up next to it. He quickly got out and made his way around the back, opening the door for Tina. "That's quite the gesture, Tillman," George said as he hopped out of the truck.

"Yeah, well. Someone's got to be around here," the cab driver replied.

George wanted to take a few steps toward him to try and intimidate him but stopped once Tina stepped out of the car. He took a step back and nearly bumped into Zoey.

"Careful!" she shouted.

Leon got out of the truck as well. "Yo! Tina! What's hangin'?"

He wanted to add *besides the obvious* but felt it was too early for sexual innuendoes.

"Not much. Just working," she said as she took her bag from Tillman who was holding it out for her.

The cab driver could feel his blood pressure rising and decided to get out of there. She paid him and he practically ran around the front of the taxi. He hopped in and quickly backed up.

"Why's he in such a hurry?" Tina asked.

"Tillman? Dude's blood pressure has gone through the roof since graduating," Leon stated.

"Wasn't he the graduating class after us?" Tina wondered.

"Yep. He's a year younger but will probably blow his top faster than any of us," Leon laughed.

Zoey approached Tina and hugged her. "It's so nice to see you."

"You too! All of you! It's been ten years too long!"

They broke away from each other but still held hands.

"You look amazing!" Zoey said.

"Look at those luscious blonde wavy curls. I wish I could get my hair to do that!" Tina said, admiring them.

"You're too kind!" Zoey said.

Tina then looked at Leon and George. "I guess the gym has become a home away from home for you boys?"

Both men blushed.

She then looked at the other cars. "Is this all that's coming?"

"I could only get six of us to go out on the boat. Don't worry though. We'll meet up with the rest at the school this afternoon," Zoey explained.

"I'm assuming the other two are inside?"

"Probably. Like you, we just got here."

"Okay then!" Tina's heart fluttered a bit. "Let's see how the last ten years has treated them."

***

"He's going to want a carcass," Joe said. "Living or dead."

Fred chuckled. "We'll hire another transporter. This time, U-Haul. Preferably one to hold a steel cage."

"You know he wants it submerged for travel."

"Then he'll need to increase the dosage. Or at least have some sedative in the water."

Joe turned to his father. The two of them had been scanning the water from a dry patch in the swamp for an hour. It was getting tiresome. "I don't know. I think we ought to just kill it."

"What the hell did you just say?"

"It's going to kill again if it hasn't already."

Fred turned and began to make his way down towards the shore. Mud caught his feet several steps of the way. Every time he pried his boot free it was accompanied by a suction sound.

"Are you crazy?" Joe cried out.

"It's not going to show its ugly head unless something draws it out." Fred placed his hand in the lukewarm water.

Joe scoffed at the idea. "You're going to get yourself killed."

"Don't lecture me on my survival rate. You sound just like your mother did."

"Low blow." Joe shook his head and then turned away.

After his son's scolding, Fred began thinking. They needed bait. If he could lure it out somehow, without him being directly in its path, that would be all the better.

"What we need is bait," Joe said aloud.

"Exactly what I was thinking."

He began to climb back up the shore when something bubbled below the bayou. His immediate reaction was to turn around. When he did, he saw frothing and an object beginning to shape below the surface. It took on the form of an object that seemed to have scales. With its body came odd patterns. The more it floated to the top, the quicker he realized what it was.

"It's a mangled deer."

Joe took a step forward. "Looks like our friend has killed something else after all."

CHAPTER FIVE

Obnoxious.

As Trent kicked back with another beer in hand, he realized how perfect his life was. He had it all. A rich father, willing to pay for anything, unlimited free time, and a hot piece dancing for him amidst the swamps of Florida. Ava was not just a real looker, she was exotic. What's more, she put up with his antics and lack of morals and embraced them. A rarity.

He often wondered if she would still stick around if he had no financial freedom. Every time the thought arose, he scoffed. *She needs me.*

Suddenly, Ava began to lower her hands towards her abdomen. She lifted her tank top and revealed her two massive, titillating breasts. The sensation he felt at the sight of them was downright poetic. He was not what one would call a girthy specimen. It was embarrassing in his youth. Not so much anymore. Not with Ava around.

They had started out as a summer fling. Actually, several women had. That very year even. She was the one who tolerated his behavior and did not care about his manhood. She was in it for the money and that was alright. As long as she looked good, that was all that mattered.

She reached down and began to rub her hand against his crotch region. He moaned loudly. She was practically a professional masseuse without having the degree or license. He almost felt himself lose it but managed to think about something else and focus on it.

"Ready for some swamp sex?" She grinned.

"You don't have to ask me twice!"

Slowly, torturously, she unzipped his fly. She reached inside his pants and grabbed him, stroking slowly. She then snuck her hand in his underwear and fished it out.

"Oh, you're so big."

He knew it was a lie, but he appreciated her effort. "It's all for you, babe."

Her tongue danced around the tip. A strand of precum dangled down her chin. She smiled as she stuffed him inside her mouth.

"Oh!" he groaned loudly.

It was something about heat that made him last longer. In the cold, this whole ordeal would have lasted a minute. He was really starting to like Florida.

After a few minutes, she wiggled herself out of her tight jeans and white underwear that had a little pink bow on top. Then, she climbed up to him, preparing for a good time. She straddled him, her hips swaying back and forth.

The more erect he got, the more she too moaned. She could not explain it. The heat, the swamp, the scenery. It all worked for her. It was the prefect vacation. She had never felt him this way before, hard and longer than what seemed to be usual. He was really turning out a solid performance. His hips rose and fell in a powerful thrusting motion. The momentum caused her to lift off him several times.

"Oh yeah, baby! Oh yeah! Oh God! Oh Gawd!"

Three long spikes punctured through her. They stuck out of her chest and midsection. Blood squirted out of each point. Entry or exit, crimson gore erupted out in a spraying fashion. It splattered onto Trent who immediately felt his manhood shrink.

Ava let out a terrible, pain-filled, gurgled scream and coughed up more of the red substance. Her eyes watered as the white-hot searing pain ran through her whole frame. She went into shock yet could feel everything. The spikes had just missed her spinal cord by mere inches.

Then, before Trent could grab at her, she was lifted off of him and hoisted into the air. She hung there, suspended over him. Ribbons of plasma rained down on him like a scarlet parade.

"Ava!" he screamed.

She began to spasm. Her body was shaking. As she retched, she felt a new sensation. It started as a slight tingling. It was like being briefly zapped when grabbing a metal rod at first. It went through her whole body. Then, the electrical current began to increase in voltage. She managed to glance down at Trent who looked horrified.

A surge of electricity ran through her whole body. She shook violently. Her eyes popped out of her skull, hair frayed and burnt away. Then, as she convulsed for the last time, she exploded into a meaty spray of gushing gore and uncoiled intestines. Pieces of her spilled down onto Trent as he watched in abject horror.

Somehow, as he watched the scene transpire before him, he returned to sanity. He quickly reached down for the engine. The long, serpentine tail slipped back into the swamp. It disappeared with barely a ripple. Trent was not about to wait for it to come get him.

Pulling the cord, the engine thankfully came to life. He placed it in the water and guided the boat in a wide U-turn. Soon, he was speeding out of there. He had to get back to the shop. He mused on what to say when he called the police.

An idea entered his mind that he was not entirely against. *I can call my dad. He'll know what to do!* He reached into his pocket to retrieve his phone. Before he could dial, the boat rocketed to the left. His phone slipped from his blood-slicked hands.

"No!"

He realized what had happened and knew it was too late. There would be no making it home. His girl was gone and so was he. He gulped, allowing tears to trickle down his cheeks. The thought of Ava clouded his mind. What had happened to her was awful. Absolutely morbid. She did not deserve the fate she received. Gone forever, Ava was more than just a summer fling. Trent began to realize he needed her more than she needed him.

It was too late.

A scaly head, followed by its long, tube-shaped body, slithered from the depths a few yards ahead of him.

"You bastard!" Trent screamed at the creature.

He suddenly felt compelled to charge at the monstrosity. As his gaze fell upon it, he realized it was not natural. It wavered there, briefly. Its twenty-foot length propelled out of the water by what he figured was another twenty feet below the surface. The scaly serpent sat suspended there. Its eyes gleamed a fiery red. The black slits narrowed on him. Its underbelly was a sickly green, almost tinted with grey. Its back was laden with blackish brown scales. What hypnotically grabbed Trent's attention were the fins on its side. It was not just some snake. It was a fish or something. Something with a crocodilian or gator head and two little legs dangling from the upper section near its head.

"What in the hell are you?" he cried out as he sped towards monstrosity.

As he approached, warning sirens went off in his head. They told him to turn back. To save his own skin. Don't die an idiot!

He had to do this. Ava was all he had in this world. The hell with the Ferrari, screw his controlling father with the deep pockets and cigar hanging from his lip at all times. Ava gave him the time of day. She was everything he needed and the thing merely ten yards in front of him had taken her away.

"I'm going to kill you!"

The creature did not move. If it were not for its eyes watching him approach, it could have been confused for a statue. One of bumps and scales. Soon, its head tilted downward as he became too close to simply look towards.

"Come get some!"

It attacked. Trent did not know how fast it had moved or when it had initiated the strike. It just happened and he was caught completely off guard. With one toothy chomp, it bit down on his head and tore it from the stump. The little motorboat never even grazed the creature as it charged back into the water and continued to search for more prey.

Trent's lifeless body sat there. His hand was still clutching the steerer of the engine. As he began to slouch over, the boat turned. Blood pumped in vigorous fashion from where his head used to be. It shot upward in a grisly geyser as well as spilled down onto his white T-shirt. His muscles relaxed as death overcame him. He unknowingly was about to run into a sandbank.

***

The first thing Tina did when she walked into Raymond's Rides was bump into Mark. It was completely unintentional. He had been standing by the bait freezer when she opened the door and knocked into him. He was taken aback at first, not sure who would run a door into him. When he turned and saw her though, all previous notions of annoyance disappeared.

"Sorry," she said suddenly.

"It happens," Mark smiled.

Zoey walked in behind Tina. She had been ignoring his texts since graduation. Ever since she hooked up with George Barkley, in fact. He was not a good man if he remembered correctly. A bad influence on all those around him. Mark nodded at her, and she smiled in return.

Speak of the devil, Mark thought as Geroge walked in behind her. He appeared to have aged fifteen years instead of ten. With his physique, one would figure he would be at least somewhat handsome. He looked unapproachable and unkempt.

Leon came in next. He was a character for sure. The Wyman cool kid. His sharp features brought out the physical labor he had gone through to get the way he looked. His muscles were positively bulging. Mark never had a problem with him until he started hanging around with George.

At the moment, Leon seemed to be looking around the shop. It was clear he was after Cecilia. She was a nice woman, pretty. A lot of baggage but she managed just fine. Mark returned his attention to Tina who was showing off her award-winning smile.

"How've you been?"

"Alright. And yourself?"

"Fabulous. I just got off a photoshoot. I had to come down here to catch up with ya'll."

"Ya'll? Would you listen to that! Your Cajun's already beginning to come in!" Leon chuckled.

"Better than yours," Mark smirked.

The two-fist pumped.

George did not partake. He was keeping an eye on Zoey as she approached the counter.

"Hey, Neil," she said.

"Hello," he said sternly. "The other one's down by the docks."

He then shuffled around the counter and made his way over towards the door. He locked it and turned back. "You folks ready?"

"Oh great, Captain Buzzkill's coming along?" Leon laughed.

"No one drives the cabin cruiser but me. You have a problem with that *ya'll* can swim to the high school." His jab at them took Zoey aback.

"We'll appreciate your company," she spoke up.

"Mmhmm. 'Bout time someone did." He made his way back behind the counter.

Looking at the key rack, he searched for the one he desired. There were not many, five to be exact. He seemed to enjoy taking his time.

George sighed. "C'mon, old man. We're ready to go!"

"Patience is a virtue." Neil smiled and picked the key off the wall.

He gave them a quick jingle and then faced the group. "Let's get this tour underway."

The docks looked in need of repair. The siding was covered in crust and shells and there was a thin sheet of slime around the edges. They shone in the mid-morning sun. Cecilia was thankful that the walkway was at least clear of mucky substances.

She was on her phone but not really paying attention to it. Her father had texted her an obscene amount of times in the last hour. She knew he thought the world of his little princess, but he was beginning to show signs of clinginess. She was a woman now. One whose looks were going to draw attention. The kind her father was afraid of.

At first, she responded to his countless texts. Now she was beginning to become annoyed. Responding with simple, one-word sentences. It was not fair to him.

He meant well but there was a line that needed to be drawn.

The door opened to the shop, and she saw Neil leading the group outside. She was impressed that Leon cleaned up so nicely. George looked unkempt. His girlfriend, Zoey, looked like the average blonde hottie. At least, average in how she perceived them. Her golden locks of wavy hair and dark piercing eyes were just some of the attributes that made her attractive. Cecilia never swung that way. At least, she did not think she did.

When Tina strode out, she was taken aback. The woman was a bombshell. Her bright, red hair hung over her shoulder in a braided ponytail. She looked over at Cecilia and smiled with her perfect pearly whites. Two big things caught her attention the most. As was probably the case for any onlooker. Breasts were breasts but hers were behemoths.

Finally, Mark came out. She had met him inside and had forgotten he had even gone to the same school as her. She did not remember crossing him in the halls. As soon as he spoke though, she figured it out. He was the first guy to ever ask her out. She had politely declined which made a lot of the other girls in her class chastise her.

Originally, she thought his proposal of dinner and a movie was a prank. There was temptation to go out with him, of course. He was a good-looking young man. The problem was her features were less than desirable to most.

She recalled a boy from the chess club asking her out too. She had said yes but he stood her up. Looking at Leon, she saw a chance with someone halfway decent. It was about time too. She was nearly in her thirties and had never had a good lay. There was that one guy down on Brockton Street that had mowed her mother's lawn for a time. He was sluggish in the sack though. She chuckled at the memory.

Neil and the group made their way onto the docks. They approached Cecilia with a variety of expressions. Neil, naturally, seemed disinterested. Leon and George seemed happy to see her again at the very least. Leon especially. Zoey was excited, as was Tina. Mark gave a smile which she returned and nodded.

She received hug after hug.

"It's been too long!" Zoey said aloud.

"That it has!" Leon took her in a bear hug.

The vice-like grip was not as harsh as she thought initially. He seemed to know just how to hold her without hurting her.

"I would give you a hug, but I saw you first," he stated.

"Well then you'll get another one." Cecilia surprised him. She was not going to let him one up her. Besides, they were young. Time changes, people change. It was all water under the bridge now.

The engine roared to life. The group looked down and saw Neil over by the consol. "Let's get your little shindig underway!"

CHAPTER SIX

Dreaming primeval.

He had done it. The ultimate predator was born into the world by way of splicing genes. Harvesting the genetic makeup was the easy part. According to Boudreaux's science team, the combining of two different species was in a whole other league. There were attempts and failures, some so spectacular that it nearly cost the life of the team.

Boudreaux remembered one night, when the current specimen was growing restless, it had smashed its way out of its holding cell and nearly killed a security guard. The man was left with third degree burns all over his body. A regular singed soul. He and his family were paid hush money. So far, there had been no fatalities.

It was not until a few days ago that that bumbling bozo, Fred Brady and his equally inept son, Joe, called in and reported the damn thing had killed an officer. The cop was in the wrong place at the wrong time. Boudreaux was willing to let the two men perform a cleanup. He was more concerned about how they were going to get it back.

The creature was thirty feet long and growing rapidly. He began to wonder if the tranquilizers would do any good.

A more perfect creature could not exist in his eyes. It was growing immune to the sedatives and was now on a rampage. The last thing Boudreaux wanted was to read a headline saying something along the lines of *Swamp Serpent on the Loose.* Or worse, *A Scientific Tragedy.*

It was no secret that he had been cutting down on staff as well as docking pay for those who could not make the adjustment to a smaller team. He was now down to three scientists. He had five three days ago. Two were relieved of duty once the cop was killed.

They claimed they had no idea. Boudreaux agreed. They were not aware of the creature's capabilities. The full potential of its bodily chemistry was alien to them. *What do I pay these guys for, to sit on their asses?*

He sat back in his leather chair and began pondering on what the next cover story would be. If things got out of hand, he would need both a solid alibi and potentially a reason as to why such a creature was made.

"It's just one big shit sandwich," he mumbled to himself.

Standing up from the cushiony seat, he walked over towards the windows. He was in a high-rise apartment. He preferred to work from home and only came in during meetings and serious situations. Neither of which he desired. As he looked out, he took in the sights below. Cars passed by with less than a little patience. He could not hear the honking, shouting, and cursing but he could imagine it. There were people, they looked like ants. Hundreds of them shambled along the sidewalk or crossed the street without so much as a curtesy wave.

"What would happen if we were suddenly thrust back in time? Back when the world was just teeth and flesh," he wondered.

He then scoffed at the idea. "Mass extinction."

The phone rang suddenly, and he strode across the room. He saw the caller ID said *Brady*. "What do they want now?"

Without hesitation, he answered. "This better be important."

"It's killed again."

"What! What do you mean?"

"I mean what I said."

"You've had almost three days to recapture this thing. What is going on out there, damnit?"

"It killed a deer."

"A deer? You got me all worried because my product killed a deer?"

"Just thought I should keep you updated."

"Do me a favor, Freddy. Don't call me again unless there is a real emergency." Boudreaux hung up and turned to face the window again.

The possible cost of Fred's actions weighed down on him. Boudreaux had been wire tapped back in the eighties. When it seemed everyone on the job wanted to be the cool one like in the movies. It was an invasion of privacy as far as he was concerned. He then remembered a line from an old movie. Something about the call coming from inside the house.

He involuntarily shuddered and made his way over to his minibar. He grabbed a shot glass and filled it with fireballs. Taking the single swig, he let it run smoothly down his throat.

Turning towards the window, he approached with a suaveness to him. He looked down again. "History is filled with horror!" He laughed manically. "Let us learn to change or suffer the call of death!"

***

Driving down the sunlit road, Tillman was beginning to regret his occupation. The transportation side of things was not his issue. The customers on the other hand were becoming more problematic with each passing day. He had dealt with his fair share of drunken partygoers and one-night stands. He even witnessed a couple's relationship end in the backseat of his cab.

The guy had saved his apparent ex-girlfriend's number that still had a heart emoji next to the name. His new fling did not buy his story one bit. Tillman made the mistake of expressing a reaction. It was a simple smirk, but it earned him a bad review and one star across the websites. Everyone had an opinion when they hid behind a keyboard.

He focused on the road ahead of him. It was not in a metaphysical sense either. The weather outside was brutal but there was a simple elegance to it. Florida had a primal mystique about it. Especially out in the swamps where countless critters lurked. He tried not to look out into the gleaming water but caught himself staring at the shining surface often. It was relaxing. His eyes away from the manmade road, he managed to catch sight of something he otherwise would have missed.

It was a small boat.

Pressing against the brake pedal slowly, he turned the yellow cab towards the side of the road. He saw an opening and parked on a grass patch. Pulling out his phone, his next scheduled pick up was in twenty minutes. It would only take approximately thirteen minutes to get there. *A lucky number,* he thought.

The door opened. He stepped out and was greeted with a wave of humidity. He began to sweat profusely. He looked over the sign that read *taxi* and saw the small watercraft. It was up against a sandbank. There was something off about the scene before him. The speedboat looked abandoned, and he could not hear anyone around. All the sounds came from stridulating crickets and croaking frogs. A random bird made a loud chirping sound that startled the cool expression off his face. His head snapped up at the trees. After realizing what it was, he lowered his head. The boat was still there, unoccupied.

Quickly looking around, he saw no one coming or going to or from his direction. There were also no sounds of some yuppie couple screwing around in the woods. It was his first assumption. People did weird things.

He decided to venture out towards the embankment. There was enough intrigue to garner at least a glimpse. Perhaps it was not abandoned. That part did not interest him. What did was what could be aboard. If someone left in a hurry, they may have forgotten some sort of personal belonging. He did not consider himself an experienced thief. Throughout his life he stole perhaps three times. Once from his aunt's seamstress business. It was a thimble. He did not know why he took it, but he did. The other two times were candy from the local convenient store.

If there was something worth taking aboard the speedboat, he wondered if he would call it right away. There was no rush. As far as he was concerned, it was finders keepers. The very thought of a potential dead body never crossed his mind.

He walked down the path. It was caked in mud and a bit overgrown. Wearing sandals definitely did not help in the mildly rough terrain. He passed the line of trees that acted as a barrier to the woods. It was not a far journey to the water's edge, though it was taking forever. Every small suction of mud or strand of uprooted vine seemed to trip him up, hampering his progress.

Mugginess surrounded him. It was hot when he got out of the air-conditioned cab. Now he was drenched from head to toe, and he had only been walking for a mere forty-five seconds. It was probably another fifteen feet from the shoreline. The boat was visible. The way it sat, he could not distinguish what was on board.

At first, he had not noticed the red stains that splattered across the interior. The initial thing he registered was a rotted smell. It was earthy in its pungency. Like someone put a garden on the bottom of the boat filled with worms and other insects. His arm immediately shot over his mouth and nose. He fought back the urge to gag.

There were times in his life he wished he was not so bold to investigate strange things. This was one of them. He was now close enough to see inside. It was a dark red mess. There was no corpse aboard but there was blood. A lot of it. A metric ton. Enough to have coated the interior almost completely. A sickly shade of crimson. He then noticed something clinging to the side closest to him. At first, it looked like grass or weed. Upon further inspection he realized with grave horror what it was.

It was a clump of matter, bloodied hair.

Releasing the strands, the jumbled mess fell into the mud. He then noticed the piece of scalp still attached.

"Nope!"

Tillman spun around and began back towards the road. This was not happening. It had to be some misunderstanding. People died out here, sure. What he saw was a mutilation. No gator nor snake could have done that. The only thing it could have been was a murder. More like butchering. Still a serious crime committed upon some poor hapless person.

Watching the ground, he made sure to walk around the general area where his feet had stepped. The indents were mostly clear. There was no reason not to play it safe though. He didn't want to break a foot and spend the night out here. While he ran, he searched for his phone. He deduced that it was in the car.

"Damnit!"

There was a lump in his vest. He reached for the pocket, praying it would be the device. He fished it out and was relieved. The very sight of the modern miracle of communication caused tears to well up in his eyes. "Thank you!"

Slowing his pace slightly, he slid his finger across the screen and waited for his face to unlock it. It failed. He tried again but with the same luck. He resorted to trying one more time. It failed and he began to type in the six-digit password. He knew it by heart, but his fingers were cramping up. The fear of what he saw stuck in the forefront of his mind.

Incorrect password.

"Fuck you!" he exclaimed.

Crack. Snap. Creak.

Tillman stopped dead in his tracks and turned towards the direction of the sound. It was coming from somewhere far off in the woods. Whatever it was, it was enough to knock some branches of something down. The aching noise indicated it was not a rotted trunk but rather a strong tree.

He began to whimper. Looking down at his phone, he began to walk again. He was visibly tense. His whole posture was rigid like a cold skeleton. Yet he moved without direction. He knew he was going straight but not about the uprooted twig that caught his foot. He was sent sprawling forward. His phone went flying from his grasp.

"No!" he shouted angrily.

There was no immediate pain. There was a shock that was quickly wearing off. His whole body was briefly numb. He managed to sit up and look down. There was the root, the mud, and his foot which was still snagged. He initially tried to pull his foot free, but it was bent at an awkward angle. He reached forward and began to try and maneuver the twig out of the way. His mind did not comprehend the sound at first. When it did, he realized there was something sliding against the ground. It made a solid crunching sound.

His foot came free, and he stood up. It did not hurt. Very lucky. For now. He saw the creature. It was some horrendous amalgamation of species he recognized but couldn't put a finger on. The sight was just too fantastic to cope with. His eyes registered one thing while his mind processed something else. This had to be a dream.

It sized him up, towering over him like a lion looking down from a cliff at its prey. He felt like a helpless rabbit. The red eyes bore into his. He moved one way, those slit-shaped pupils followed. There was an understanding between predator and prey. It was going to kill him, and he had no chance. They both knew it. The trouble Tillman was having was accepting it. He raised his arm slowly, holding out his hand.

"Please don't," he begged.

As if being served food on a platter, the creature swiftly yet carefully bit down around his elbow. It had been so gentle that the searing flash of agony did not register at first. Tillman screamed a full three seconds after it had bitten him. Then, it gave a twist and severed his arm.

Bringing what was left of his bodily extension to his side, his other hand clutched around the stump. He felt the warm blood and nub of bone. The pain was white hot. He turned and began to run back to his cab. Hearing the creature gulp and swallow his arm was enough to make him pass out and that was already after the blood loss. His vision was growing foggy. It looked like someone smeared gel onto his organic camera. Before he knew it, he bumped into the side of the cab.

He did not want to relinquish his injured body part but managed to reach for the door handle.

He was inside the cab within a few seconds. The keys were in his pocket on his left side. He had to reach over with his right arm to grab them. It took precious seconds. He put the keys in the ignition and started it.

Suddenly, everything died. He looked out and saw a tail with three spikes pressing against the passenger side door. There was no choice now. He had to get out and run. He was not sure how much more he could take. He pulled the door handle and was immediately greeted with shock after shock of an electrical current. His body was riddled with a new, ignited pain. It seemed to surge through him. Much like the brief fear he experienced when falling down in the swamp. Except this was prolonged. The throes of agony were intense. He shook his body in a way that would put Elvis Presley to shame.

Then, he exploded. Chunks of gore scattered about. Intestines slipped down onto the ground. His eyeballs popped and brains splattered against the window.

Much like the job he was growing sick of, he was done for good.

CHAPTER SEVEN

Boom!

The engine aboard the tour boat kicked to life. It was a horrible, guttural noise. Mark was surprised the thing even came on. He was quite savvy with mechanical equipment and figured the trip would end before it could start. Part of him was overjoyed that the engine kicked on. The other side of him secretly wanted it to stall and maybe he could hook up with Tina back in town.

Seeing Cecilia was probably the biggest turn-off he could have experienced. She was snooty in her nerd years, and she seemed to not have changed much. He was a bit passive aggressive, he had admitted to himself. Maybe she changed more than just her appearance.

Zoey was the hardest hit. They had dated briefly back in high school. Things were good between them. He had never really understood why it ended but it did, nevertheless. It had been ten years, after all.

The boat puttered along. A loud chugging sound could be heard from the engine. It was likely to scare off any wildlife. Not that anyone was complaining too much. No need to run into alligators or snakes out here. Especially if swimming was in their plans.

It was going to be a fun trip.

Cecilia was standing by the railings at the stern. She watched as the glistening water shimmered across the green surface. High sitting aquatic plants practically stuck out. Seaweed, kelp, lily pads. It was a swamp alright. Still, there was admiration to be had.

Another form of admiration approached her. Leon Tate joined her by the guardrail. He smiled and she gave a sheepish grin.

"Beautiful, isn't it?"

"It's definitely something." She glanced out at the water.

He paused. "So how have you been? I didn't see you around much after high school."

"Or during," she added.

"Oh, hey. It's my fault. I should've been more mature about my feelings for you."

"You had feelings for me?" she chuckled.

"What? Can't a guy have misunderstood affections for one of his classmates?"

She pondered for a moment. "I guess."

Facing the swamp again, Cecilia seemed distant. "You know, I wasn't very fair to those who showed any inkling of attraction to me in the past."

"It's alright. We were young and stupid."

"I always just thought it was a prank. Like I was some big joke."

Leon felt something in that moment. Initially, he just wanted to get in her pants. It seemed like a fool proof plan. She was obviously yearning for someone. Now that she was being coy and playing hard to get, he began to see why. It all came from fear.

"I didn't know."

"None of you did."

He paused. "Maybe we should have."

Leon turned and made his way back to his seat.

It was Cecilia's turn to be impressed. She thought of Leon as nothing more than a ravenous hound, searching for his next play toy. The vulnerability that accompanied his angst was unexpected to say the least. Still, she never broke eye contact with the swamp.

Tina was having a hard time not looking at Mark. He was more rugged than last she saw of him. Yet, there was a sadness in his eyes she could not place. Something was clearly weighing him down. Whether or not it was her business, she would not pry. She was just happy to see him.

He had clearly noticed her casual glances and had regarded them cooly. He was not tense or nervous. Perhaps a bit cocky but not in that irritating way where one thought they were better than everyone else. Tina tried to compose herself. There was the idea that he should make the first move, but he did not seem to be in a hurry.

It was clear he was a bit more experienced than other men in the art of flirting. She had heard the rumors about his manhood and was curious. There was more to him though. She wanted to know what made him so mysterious.

Unexpectedly, he stood up and made his way over. Her heart began to flutter as she stared up at him. His walk was assertive, he was in perfect control of his body. It was a good sign. He knew himself well. Some guys she had been with were lacking in several departments. The biggest self-control.

Mark took a seat next to her. Her pale cheeks gave way to blushing. It was impossible to disguise it. He tried to appear as if he did not notice but it was clear as day.

"How've you been?" he asked.

"I've been good." She smiled. "Just living the dream."

"Oh?" he inquired.

"I do modeling." She waited for the astonished look or suggestive remark.

"Ya must visit a lot of cool places."

She grinned. "I've visited Canada, Ireland, and am currently doing a photoshoot in Hawaii."

"That's awesome."

"Yeah." She couldn't help her obnoxious tone. The word came out over-exasperated.

"I've always wanted to visit Hawaii."

"It's a nice place to just relax," she told him. "What about you? What have you been up to?"

"I do odd jobs here and there. There seems to be a lot of those here."

"Yeah. I remember you were quite the football enthusiast."

"Eh. I was never really that good."

"Are you kidding! Those chumps would have never won a game without you."

He chuckled. "I don't know about that."

"I remember you running for a hundred fifty yards and making a touchdown. Who else did that during their time?"

"You remember that?" His eyebrow arched.

"I was a cheerleader, remember?" she giggled.

"Oh yeah! You never missed a game!"

"I did once. We had to put my family pet down. That was hard."

Mark nodded. "It's tough."

"Do you have any pets?" she asked.

"A dog."

"Good. I can't stand cats," she stated.

"Sounds like you and I will get along great then." He smiled.

Zoey had been transfixed by the glistening weeping willows that hung low enough to touch the surface of the swamp. Just as they passed them, the sun beamed from behind creating a shine that was captivating. She had always been rather oblivious to nature. Being wrapped up in her own problems, she often forgot just how majestic everything was. Even out in a swamp.

George seemed to feel the same way but had a different response. He inched closer to Zoey and placed a hand on her knee. She tried to ignore him, but his hand kept sliding higher on her leg.

"Beautiful day," he said.

"Yep," she said coldly.

"How far is this place we're going?"

"About an hour ride."

"A lot can happen in an hour," he said, interest piqued.

"Enjoy the scenery."

"Don't worry, I am." His hand released its hold on her.

Neil sensed there was hostility from the couple. Not that he cared all that much. It was their business. Still, he sat up in the consol and did nothing but look out for any sticks or other wooden debris he might bump into.

The swamp had its charm, but it was weighing down on him like a sauna. Or a hot cloth over his whole body. The abundant insects were acupuncture but made you itch instead of feeling relaxed. He was not sure how much more of his homemade bug repellent he had left. He made a mental note to make more when he got back. The cannister he had was half empty.

The more he sweat, the more it came off. There was no way around it. He was tempted to buy one of those portable neck fans that he saw on some website. He was not sure how good they worked and was not about to drop over twenty bucks on one.

He would just deal with it.

Casually glancing down on the deck, he saw everyone coupled off. The red head in the middle was attractive but way out of his league. Too young as well. This may have been their reunion but he had missed every get together he had had with Wyman High. He never saw the point. No one liked him then.

Looking at her again though, reminded him of a teacher he had. Same face, same bright red hair color. *Maybe it was her daughter?* he thought as he returned his attention ahead. The swamp was noticeably absent of clustered branches. He knew all the spots to avoid. Rocks that stuck out like icebergs made of stone, critters that did not much like anything or anyone else's presence. It was a tricky area, but he knew it well. He dared another look down at the woman on deck.

She looks just like her. Slightly prettier too. He recalled the science class she taught. There was no other class he passed. Everyone wondered why, especially because he hated science. They never found out about the little crush he had on his fiery-haired teacher.

George made his way up the ladder. The deck below was beginning to bore him. Zoey was too. She had not put out like she used to in the past. Now she was becoming a regular prude. He stood near the consol. Neil's eyes shifted. He was clearly trying to avoid him.

"Nice boat."

"Mmm," he grumbled in response.

"Isn't it a bit large for a swamp?" George inquired.

"Not if you know how to drive it."

"I do actually. My dad used to take us out on the river canals in a boat a little smaller than this."

Neil ignored Geroge as he prattled on. "Me and him, we would be on the water for hours. I finally learned how to captain the boat when I was a teenager."

"Interesting."

"I haven't been on a boat since he died though."

"Understandable."

"Mind if I give her a steer?" George asked a little too perkily.

This got Neil's attention. "Like I told your girly friend. No one drives this here cabin cruiser but me."

"I'll be careful. I promise!"

"Get back on the deck before I turn this boat around," Neil snarled.

"Alright. Alright. Sheesh. There's no need to be such a grouch." George turned and made his way back down the ladder.

Zoey was at the bottom waiting for him. She had a smile on her face as if she was satisfied. George wanted to smack the grin off her rosy cheeks but decided against it.

"Making friends?" she said with a chipper tone.

"Blow me." He marched back over toward his spot.

The cushioned seat was hot. They had been in the shade when they left. Now that they were out in the open, everything was heating up and he was miserable. He wanted to get up again. Maybe take a dip. Perhaps an alligator would get him. *That'd wipe the cheeky smile off her dumb face.*

***

It hung there, lifeless. The hair was matted as crimson spots covered sections of its tan coat. Mangled and torn, the deer was suspended over the ground by a few feet. Insects swarmed all over the gory carcass.

They invaded its body, inside and out. They entered through its mouth and exited out empty eye sockets. It rectum was a nesting ground for future flies.

Joe was beginning to feel woozy at the very smell of the dead mammal, let alone the sight of it. He wanted to cut it down and continue the hunt. His father seemed to think this was the best way to lure out the creature.

"Stop fidgeting," Fred told his son who had covered his nose for the umpteenth time.

"This is disgusting."

"Then go. Walk away and come back when you're ready to be a man."

"You don't have to be rude," Joe said as he attempted to release his grip on his nostrils.

A sudden faint breeze wafted the pungent odor over their way. He gagged loudly.

"Shut it, boy!" Fred whispered sternly.

Joe could not believe the obscene stench the dead animal was producing. What's worse was it carried a wet dog smell from being in the swamp. He turned and looked out in the woods. A change of scenery might help to calm his nerves. Or so he thought.

It was there. Fifty yards out, in a clear path. The area had been open enough so that it would not snap any sticks under its immense girth. He had not had a good look at the creature before it took that cop and disappeared with him into the swamp. Seeing it now was something straight out of a nightmare. Or a lab.

He absentmindedly reached up for his father. Tugging on his flannel sleeve, the man attempted to shrug him off.

"D, dad," he said softly.

"I told you to be quiet!" Fred snapped at him.

"I think it already knows we're here."

Fred went rigid at that point. He then slowly turned around and looked down at his son. He was pointing towards something in the woods. He followed the direction out and saw it. The creature was slowly inching towards them. The trees between them somewhat obstructed the view but it was there. No doubt.

"Don't move," Fred said quietly.

He sat there, frozen. The creature, however, did start to motion towards them. It slowly picked up speed as it let loose a low, guttural roar. It sounded like an organic car engine.

Neither man budged. In the back of Fred's mind, he was impressed at his son's willingness to stare death in the face and not run. He chalked it up to him being paralyzed with fear. There was no other way.

Methodically, Fred raised the tranquilizer gun. He stopped every few inches when the creature's red eyes focused on them. Then, when they darted away, he raised it again. Soon enough, it was near his midsection. He did not want to hip fire at the thing but there was not much choice.

Then, the creature pulled a maneuver that neither was expecting. Joe was relieved while Fred, annoyed. It slithered in a wide half-circle and made its way around them. The deer carcass became its new target. Once the serpentine-like anomaly was close enough, the bloated body was investigated.

It bumped and sniffed the deer. There seemed to be a recollection there. It had indeed already killed this prey. Something was appetizing to it though. As if it being waterlogged added an extra stimulating seasoning to its aroma.

Parting its jaws, it bit down around the deer's stomach. Its stomach popped like a water ballon, spilling its contents onto the ground. An instant later and the entire body came apart.

Joe fought the urge to gag. His eyes watered. He was still facing away but the perfume of death lingered over him like a green stench cloud. Covering his mouth with his hands, bile began to build up in his throat. Vomit began spraying through his barely parted fingers. Fred turned to see this and shook his head.

"Amateur," he scoffed.

When he looked back, the deer's body was gone. As was the creature.

"Shit!" he cursed sharply.

CHAPTER EIGHT

Clear water and mind.

George Barkley had to admit he was impressed. At first sight of the inlet, he feared the worst. The whole ride up to the river was murky. Not a tropical paradise as Zoey had described it. The further they traveled down, the more the sediment became less cloudy. It almost seemed impossible.

Cecilia found it fascinating. She ran hypotheses in her head but could not figure out why the water was so clear in this particular region of the swamp. It was some kind of marvel.

Birds chirped excessively; frogs croaked deeply. Yet there was peace and harmony. The sun was peeking through the trees as if it were trying to get a glimpse into this magical place. The inlet was the only way in and out. Yet it felt secure and safe enough to reside in for all to thrive.

Zoey felt proud of herself. There was another reason she picked Neil to take them out. He not only helped her with her car but to learn about this magical place. It was something straight out of a dream, complete with the hazy filter. It shone with brilliance and envy. A hidden paradise.

She would not be surprised if it formed from a painter's imagination. Some unknown talent that could project their subconscious into the real world and create astonishing works of life.

"What is this place?" Mark was clearly taken aback. He had been through the swamp a lot during his clutter removal gigs. He would often break down dams or blockages for a fee.

"I think I'm in heaven," Leon said.

"Neil calls it Calming Cove," Zoey stated. "I have only thought about what this place looked like. It's exceeded beyond my expectations."

"You folks better get used to this spot. We're going to be here all day," Neil called down to them.

Tina stood up. "Is there a bathroom I can change in?"

"It's tight but manageable," Neil said as he slowed the cabin cruiser to a stop.

Cecilia and Tina grabbed their small bags and hurried into the deck below. Zoey did not budge. George was staring daggers at her. Mark noticed but chose not to say anything. It really was not his place. He wanted to but figured it was not the right time or place.

Leon quickly stripped down to his whites and made his way over to the starboard side. Looking down, he was amazed by the bedazzling sight below. The water glistened as if diamonds floated on the surface.

"How is this possible?" he asked.

"I looked into it," Zoey began. "Apparently the cove is surrounded by dense woods. So dense that the wind doesn't really come through much. At the inlet, there are also thick trees and brush. This part of the swamp doesn't really have high winds regardless. I guess the current isn't strong either."

"Only one way to find out." Leon smiled and dove masterfully into the water.

"Ten out of ten, buddy!" George called after him.

When he surfaced, he looked like he had experienced the best shower of his life. "You guys have to get in here!"
"Oh. Um," Zoey started.

"That's okay. We're good for now." Geroge looked back at her.

She had indeed brought a swimsuit. Having planned the whole trip, she was excited to swim in the crystal-clear lagoon. It had been her idea from the get go.

Turning down George's advancement was the icing on the cake for him. It may have been hot, but they were going to suffer through it together. He smiled at her sinisterly. It reassured his attitude towards her and the whole situation.

"C'mon, man."

George turned back to Leon. "I said we're good."

Leon did not like the bitter tone but figured he would call him out on it later. He then saw Mark peeling off his khaki shorts and white T-shirt. He was down to his underwear now. There was no hiding it anymore.

"Holy shit, man!" Leon shouted.

George did not look. If he did, he was sure Leon would get a good laugh chastising him. Instead, he turned to Zoey who was already facing the other direction. *That's right.*

"Let's cut the crap," Mark said as he reached for his briefs. "It's paradise after all."

Pulling them down, even Leon was jealous. Mark then tossed them aside and dove into the water with a better performance than Leon's.

"Oh my!" Cecilia exclaimed.

The sight of Mark's bare rump was enough to cause her to blush. She noticed Leon was still donning his underwear. If anything, he was more modest.

Leon looked at Cecilia. Her yellow bikini looked dazzling against her dark skin. Her pixie hair cut had a little butterfly bow tucked in on the side. Her cute nature made him want to hold and comfort her. Take away all the stuff done to her in high school.

She turned and looked at Zoey and George. Neither acknowledged her. She could sense that both of them were at odds. At least, for the time being. She then climbed up on the pulpit and dove feet first into the water.

Mark was already a ways out. The lukewarm lagoon felt great on his skin. He had not been skinny dipping in a long time. At least not since sophomore year. Tammy Topher had been with him then. They did not end things well. He secretly hoped she would not be at the reunion.

He spun around in the water and looked back at the cabin cruiser. She was there. Tina Bessy was wearing a dark green metallic halter swimsuit that shone just as much as her hair and smile. It also appeared she applied more of that rosy lipstick that accentuated her features. She barely seemed to fit in this bikini top but that had not aroused him most. He just wanted to be near her. See what she was like. If she was as down to earth as people had made her out to be.

Her blue eyes regarded him cooly. She did not want to draw too much attention but that had already failed. Leon was focusing on Cecilia the best he could. Cecilia had her back to him as she tread water. Tina figured she should get in. Make it easier for him.

She swung her long legs over the side and slipped in.

Neil watched intensely as Tina went into the water. She was beyond gorgeous. He seemed to have been under some kind of trance until she disappeared below. Snapping out of it, he looked around. No one seemed to have noticed. He gave a silent thanks to the man upstairs and began to rummage through the compartment below the consol.

"Now where's that damned bug spray?"

***

She had grown restless. Waiting on the police to solve the case was not getting her anywhere. His friends in law enforcement were not willing to go above the sheriff's head to investigate a case being delegated to the FBI.

Kathy Wisner had been a wreck for days. Following the efforts of the search party and the lack of signs given to his whereabouts, she figured he had run off with another woman. Their marriage was going downhill, and they both knew it. She was not as chipper and young as she used to be. Jordon, at the very least, tried to keep in shape.

It baffled her to think he was actually missing. The hunt for him had taken officers up and down his patrolling route. They went down every available pathway, looked through the marshlands on the side of the road.

The only thing of note was a vehicle that kept passing by. It was a truck with California license plates. It was once reported having been seen with a trailer attached. It had been unhitched the second time the truck was seen. There were apparently two men inside. The driver was younger than the other fellow. They could have passed for father and son.

One thought kept crossing Kathy's mind. She wondered why no one was investigating the vehicle or its occupants. It was not until Wednesday morning that she found out why.

The truck belonged to Mr. Boudreaux's company. He was settled in California but had set up shop in several places around the country including Montana, Texas, California, and Florida. It was all public information that she had gathered. Now she was starting to suspect other things.

She dug deeper and found Boudreaux's company dealt with biology and genetic makeup. They had tested certain parts of donated animal cadavers. It was a glorified pharmaceutical company where they tested on already dead animals? Something did not sit right with Kathy.

Thankfully, she had a mutual friend of hers and Jordon's. Trudy Fawn worked for the DEA office in Montana and was close enough to one of Boudreaux's company offices to have heard the stories.

On a day like any other, Kathy reached out to Trudy who seemed distraught in her own right. It was understandable. They were all friends. Kathy wanted answers, as did Trudy.

Over the next few days, they kept in touch. Trudy visited Boudreaux's office on a Thursday morning. She did not get much intel but was on edge enough to come out to Florida. Kathy was appreciative but worried.

She tried to get more information, but Trudy reassured her all would be revealed soon. Kathy just had to put her faith and trust in her. It was something she was comfortable with, even if Trudy was not. She was more than a little upset about Jordon's disappearance. Their time together was full of vigorous passion.

Longing to see him like the Montana skies every night, she wanted him again. To have him near. She felt bad for Kathy, but she had let herself go. Jordon needed someone who could keep up with him.

When the plane landed and she made it to her hotel room, she realized how humid it was in Florida. Even with the air conditioning unit at full blast. She knew it was musky, but this was nearly unbearable. She was already missing her home. Montana was just amazing even during the colder months.

Making her way out into the lobby, she saw Kathy sitting on one of the cushioned seats. She was dressed in a gown that was twice her size. Trudy nearly cringed at the sight. She had gained a significant amount of weight since their last meet up.

"Oh, thank goodness you've come!" Kathy's grin was just as unwelcoming. Her yellow stained teeth were bad enough but there was an apparent gunk built up along the gums.

"Sorry I couldn't get here sooner."

Kathy reached out to hug her. Trudy nearly gagged. She reeked of poor hygiene. She forced herself to give her a quick embrace. When they broke apart, Trudy felt like she needed to get in the shower promptly.

"Is there anything new you can tell me?"

"Not at the moment, no. I will be heading out into the swamp tomorrow."

"You'll need a guide."

"I have a compass."

Kathy gave a hearty laugh. "Are you familiar with Florida, like at all?"

"I'm a country girl, Mrs. Wisner."

"This ain't like your version of country. You'll need a guide."

Trudy quickly dug into her purse. She fished out a small device. It looked like one of those portable brick-shaped cellphones from the nineties.

"This is a tracker. I'll keep it in my backpack. With it, I have an earpiece. You can tell me which way to head and follow my progress with this." She pulled out a smaller device.

Flicking a switch, a small screen lit up. It was a video camera.

"It's connected to my headset. You can watch where I am going and guide me through the terrain."

"I haven't been in that part of the swamp before. Is there another way?" Kathy wondered.

"Then forget the camera and just keep me close to the tree line. You can switch the camera feed to a digital tracker."

"God bless technology!" Kathy cheered.

"I'll find out what happened," Trudy stated. "We'll get to the bottom of this."

"Thank you." Kathy's eyes began to water.

Trudy smiled. "Well, I hate to cut this meeting short but I have a lot of work to do."

"Okay. What time are you heading out?"

"In an hour or so. I want to head out so I have enough time before it gets dark." Trudy turned and began to make her way back to the elevator.

"Text me when you head out!"

"I'll call."

"No. Text. I'd feel better about it."

The tone in her voice was weird. Almost as if she was afraid of being seen on camera. Trudy felt bad for her briefly and nodded. "I'll text you before one o' clock."

"Delightful!" Kathy clapped her hands together and made her way out of the lobby.

The ride up the elevator was fine but when she stepped out onto the carpeted hallway, she realized she forgot to ask Kathy if she was comfortable handling the equipment. She reached for her phone but thought otherwise. More conversing with Kathy was not what she needed at the moment. She figured she could go over it with her. For now, she needed to set some things up.

CHAPTER NINE

Consequences.

While Mr. Boudreaux was clearly thinking of how much of a PR disaster it could be, Fred was more concerned about the repercussions of working for the man. He had heard horror stories of employees getting canned and then disappearing months later. Some suggested there was a big conspiracy taking place. It had to be up to twelve former workers who had *sudden accidents,* to quote the reports.

Joe seemed clueless about the whole thing. Doing some digging, Fred found a wealth of information on those who died. Car crashes, exploding homes, burning remains found. It all seemed a bit convenient that they died in flame. It was as if Boudreaux wanted to clear any potential evidence, incinerate to terminate, or both.

It made him more than uncomfortable. The worst part was, he had only scratched the surface. He did not delve too far into it. There was always the possibility of one keeping tabs on him.

As he took another drag of his cigarette, the nicotine nostalgically bringing back that sweet, savoring sense of calm, he turned to his son. Joe was sitting on a rock that looked rather misshapen. It was clear he was struggling to get comfortable. Fred looked over and saw another rock further away.

"Why don't you sit over there?"

"We need to stick together," Joe said flatly.

"Funny, you never did before."

"Did what?" Joe's head snapped in his father's direction.

"Stick together."

He was taken aback. "How fucking dare you!"

"I'm just speaking the truth."

"No, you're speaking your mind."

"Same thing."

"I ought to get you a shirt saying *boss man* or *one upper*. Or just plain *asshole*."

Fred blew a plume of smoke. "Cry me a river, boy."

Joe stood up and turned, facing him directly. "Do you understand what's going on here?"

"Do you?"

"I understand enough!" Joe continued. "We're close to the main road. Let's just get out of here. There's no reason to risk our lives for this. Mom will never forgive you or herself if something happened to either one of us."

"Your mother is a fruit cake."

Waving his father off, Joe began to walk away.

"Where are you going?"

"I'm going to flag someone down. I need to get out of this swamp. The heat is killing me."

He took two steps and then heard a click. Slowly, he looked over his shoulder and his worst nightmare became reality. His father was pointing his pistol at him.

"What. The fuck. Are you doing?" Joe said slowly.

"You don't get it, kid. You go, you die. At least if I shoot you, your death will be quick."

"Are you insane!" he exclaimed.

"Listen, son. They will come for you if you leave. They're creative. They might just give you a slow demise as opposed to quick and painless."

"Who're they?"

"Don't play dumb. Our employer has a lot of connections."

"So, they'll assassinate us?"

"They'll kill you for sure. Me, I'm seeing this mission through."

Joe stood there for a moment. Clearly in shock. Then, a calm came over him. Fred could not figure out the sudden change in expression, but it was concerning.

"Like you said, a quick death is definitely the better alternative," he said then made his way up towards the road.

"I'm warning you!" Fred shouted.

"Save it!" Joe said and then stopped dead in his tracks. "Do you see that?"

"What?" Fred took a step closer.

"It looks like a car parked on the side of the road."

Fred did not holster his weapon but rather lowered it as he approached his son. He then followed his line of view towards the wood line. There was definitely a vehicle there. It had not been there long judging by the lack of overgrowth. Something was off about it though.

The two men approached slowly. The weapon still lowered, Fred kept both hands on it. He was prepared for anything. Upon closer inspection, they saw the windows had a dark tint of red splattered all over them. Only one window was broken, or rather smashed in.

Closer now, the smell was abhorrent. It made Joe gag again.

Fred placed a hand on his shoulder. "Just stay back."

His son did as he was told.

At first, Fred was surprised at the lack of a carcass. Then he realized why. It was still there, just in tiny chunks and small sections. The poor man, or woman, exploded. Their body had ruptured like a kernel popping into popcorn.

"Shit!" he cursed.

"What is it?"

"We've got a casualty on our hands."

"Another one?" Joe turned away, his face disheveled. He then looked up and saw a boat on the embankment not too far away.

"Maybe more," he then stated.

Fred turned and saw his son was looking out over by the water.

"For fuck's sake." He marched down towards the creek.

Joe kept a distance away. His idea of sticking together wearing off ever since his dad pulled a gun on him.

"I'm going to have to call this in," Fred said as he reached for his cellphone.

"Can we call off the mission now?"

"No! Screw that! I'm going to ask for more money!" Fred scoffed at the idea of retreating.

***

The playlist kicked on with *Counting Stars* by One Republic. Zoey had tried to find the perfect songs that were popular during their high school years and the tune had been at the very top. After setting the Bluetooth speaker down on the transom, she retrieved some deflated innertubes from her bag. She then began to apply air to them.

As she did, she looked over at George who was brooding while leaning against the starboard side. *He has been annoyed with the very idea of a reunion right from the get-go. The least he could do is show some appreciation,* she thought.

His eyes glanced out at the water every so often. She hoped he was rethinking about taking a dip. It was incredibly humid. Instead, he just continued to look back down at the deck.

With one innertube down, she tossed it over the side. Leon caught it and gave it to Cecilia. He helped her on, managing to feel her smooth calf but did not press his luck. He respected the rest of her body. Still, she looked awkward while trying to climb atop it.

"Remember the time Ms. Crane fell off that chair?" Mark asked.

"She laughed the whole way back to her seat," Tina giggled.

"Yeah." Cecilia gave a quick huff as she settled in the innertube. "She always had good spirits."

"You should have seen her," Leon laughed at the memory. "She looked like she wanted to dance."

"Yeah, Mr. Ronald had come in to see if she was okay," Tina said.

"Oh, they be crushin'," Leon said.

"Mhm. They denied it but everyone knew it was true," Cecilia added.

"Principal Powers would never allow it. No mingling amongst the staff," Tina scoffed at the notion.

"Mr. PP was the biggest prude there," Leon laughed.

Zoey wanted to add that Principal Powers was also the biggest creep there. She could not count how many times he supposedly accidentally walked into the girl's bathroom. George would probably not approve of it though. *Screw it.*

"He also had to use the bathroom, like a lot."

George shot her a glance.

"You mean the girl's bathroom?" Tina added.

"Is he still alive?" Leon asked.

"I think he's still principal too," Zoey said while looking directly at George.

"Well, we'll have to keep an eye on him tonight," Mark said.

"Mhm," Leon said in agreement.

The second tube was inflated and Zoey tossed it overboard. Leon grabbed it and was about to push it over to Mark. He grabbed it and brought it over to Tina.

"That's alright," Tina smiled. "We don't need it."

She held up her pointer finger and beckoned Mark towards her with it.

He responded by pushing the black floating ring over towards Leon. He gave a whoop as he watched them make their way further from the boat.

"You guys might want to stick close to the boat."

"We'll be fine. Right, Neil?"

Neil held his hand high with a thumbs up.

"It's alright. We'll give you two some privacy," George called out to them.

Zoey shot him a glare. He just smiled.

Check and mate, he thought.

As if to add insult to injury, *Love Me Again* by John Newman came on.

A feeling came over Cecilia. The dance track was something worth getting down to. She was not going to let Leon get her so easy, but she could put on a show for him. She waited for the chorus and reached up for the string on her yellow bikini top. He noticed instantly.

"Oh hell yeah!" Leon cheered.

It came undone and she tossed it to Leon. He caught it in midair. She then began to shake her breasts right in front of him.

Leon was absorbed in them. They were round but not obnoxiously huge. Enough to get a handful of but not suffocating. He wanted to reach out but fought the urge.

The sun peeked through the trees as *Why Don't You and I* by Carlos Santana blared through the swamp. Alex Band's unique vocals enchanted the flow with control and power.

"He always had such a deep voice for a small dude," Mark chuckled.

"He was an anomaly for sure." Tina looked at him.

Both tread water, looking at each other longingly. Tina then broke her stare and looked behind him. "I may not be a prude, but I would like some privacy if we're going to do this."

Mark turned around and saw half a large tree sticking out of the water. He then held out his hand and she took it. The chorus kicked on and he mouthed the words. She giggled as they made their way behind the old chunk of wood.

She quickly pressed him against it. He was relieved it did not break. Then he yelped in surprise as she grabbed him. She stroked his shaft.

"It's a little shorter than I imagined," she said sadly.

"It's a bit cold in here. There's too much shade around."

"Well then, let me warm it up." She slipped underwater and placed his girth inside her mouth.

"Oh shit," Mark gulped.

***

Fred and Joe were at a loss for words. Joe knew his father had to call it in. He secretly wanted to watch his father feel inferior to someone else. Deep down, he felt sorry for the man. He was clearly stressed, and he was his father after all. Fred, on the other hand, was anticipating the call. He looked forward to it with bated breath. He was about to ask for double his fee.

He searched for Boudreaux's number under the contacts. Then, without hesitation, he clicked on it. It rang only once.

"Please tell me you have some good news."

"I'm afraid not. It's killed at least two people. Three if you count the cop. I'm not sure. There may have been another. Not sure, pretty messy."

"Son of a bitch!" Boudreaux exclaimed. *"What am I paying you for?"*

"We still have no witnesses. At least, not any surviving ones," Fred continued. "I can handle this. I am going to have to raise my rate though."

"Fuck you, Fred! You're not getting more than our agreed price."

"Then I guess we'll head out. Back home that is."

"I'm not going to buckle. I have plenty of other men just waiting to take your places," Boudreaux continued. *"Just so you remember, our agreement was on the safe transport of this creature. If you don't deliver, I'm not paying you squat."*

"Listen," Fred spoke sternly. "You don't double my rate and your men will have lost a great deal of time and energy searching for the thing. We're hot on its trail. They'll have to start from scratch."

There was a pause. Then a slight chuckle on the other end. *"You're currently near the road. About a hundred yards from the swamp. There seems to be a parked car and boat nearby."*

Fred did not answer.

"Bring me the creature. Or you can forget about our deal."

A clicking sound came through from the other end. Then the dial tone kicked on.

"Shit!" Fred spat. "How does he know where we are?"

"He's probably got some tracker on us," Joe suggested.

"Bull! All the equipment is ours."

"Except for that tranquilizer gun. It's been modified by the company."

Fred held the weapon against his chest. "Those bastards!"

"It's actually not a bad idea. I have a feeling the tracker is meant for the creature though. It just happens to be picking us up because we have it."

"I have three more tranquilizers." Fred looked at his son. "What do you think?"

At first, Joe was taken by surprise by his father's reliance on him. "I… I don't know. Maybe we can ditch them and switch to our guns."

"Nonsense. No live creature. No pay."

Joe thought for a minute and then reached out for the weapon. "Let me see it."

"Why?" Fred took a step back.

"I'm going to try to get the tracker off the sedative. When we put it to sleep, we'll call it in. We'll only give the location if he agrees to pay more."

Fred smirked. "It's a good thing you spend all that time fidgeting around with those gadgets."

"It's a hobby."

"It takes up most of your time," Fred stated.

"Did you want me to fix our problem or not?" Joe asked.

Reluctantly, Fred gave the gun to his son who quickly got to work.

CHAPTER TEN

A gut feeling.

Zoey sat on the transom with her arms crossed. The reunion was going from fun to dismal fast. It was all thanks to George. His demeanor and attitude were affecting everything around her. She could not even face him. The venomous looks he gave were enough to make her blood run cold.

Tina and Mark had disappeared somewhere further out in the lagoon for some alone time. She could not blame Mark. She had not handled the breakup well. She had broken it off and did not consider how he felt about it. George seemed fascinating at the time. A regular bad boy. She was a young, clueless student of love.

George then hollered with laughter. Zoey dared a look and saw that Leon was teasing Cecilia. She tried to reach for her bikini top, but he kept pulling it away at the last minute. *Why are boys so annoying?*

She took a deep breath and stood up. Then, she descended into the cabin below. There was too much testosterone in the air. Taking a seat on one of the cushions, she began to sulk. Her whole demeanor changed as a single tear fell from her cheek.

"Some plan this was," Zoey told herself. "How could I have been so dumb?"

Placing her hands over her face, she did not hear Geroge come down the steps.

"Maybe you should stick to being a homebody?"

"I don't know how much more of this I can take!" she blurted out.

The sudden outburst took George by surprise. He felt himself getting heated, his blood pressure rising. "I'm not holding you back. You want to walk out, then go!"

"You'll stop me!"

"You'd like that, wouldn't you?"

"You're sick." She stood up.

George suddenly became uncomfortable. "C'mon. There's no reason to make a scene. Not out here."

"Fuck you!" she shouted.

He held up his hands in a calming motion. "Chillax, babe."

"Don't call me that!"

"Well, I mean," he paused. "I have every right to call you that."

"Not anymore!"

His fists clenched into a tight ball. "You're nothing without me."

"I'm nothing *with* you. At least this way, I'll be rid of you!" Tears were now streaming down her face.

"You only did this trip to get with Mark. Didn't you?"

"I did it because I don't have a social life. You took that away from me!"

"You don't need one. You've got me."

"Not anymore!" she snapped at him.

George was dumbfounded at first but then turned and stormed out of the cabin. Zoey plopped onto the seat. Her sobs soon turned into laughter. She felt free for the first time in a long time.

"Everything good, bro?" Leon looked as his friend walked out onto the deck. He seemed distraught, lost, alone.

At first, George did not want to indulge him. It would be a sign of weakness. He took a deep breath and exhaled, composing himself. “It’s all good.”

“Sure doesn’t sound like it,” Cecilia stated.

“Leon,” he turned to his friend. “Keep her in line.”

“What?” Cecilia was taken aback by the snide comment.

“Dude, what’s the deal?” Leon began to swim towards the boat.

He just shook his head. “Pack it up. We’re leaving.”

Neil’s ears perked up. George turned to face him. “Is that alright, Captain?”

“You don’t have to tell me twice.”

“No!” Zoey protested. “We can’t; I planned this trip. I paid for it. We’re staying!”

“You don’t get to tell me what we’re doing!” George took a step towards her.

“Cool it!” Cecilia shouted.

“Mind your own business!” George snapped in her direction.

Zoey saw this as her chance. “You heard her! Cool off!”

With a hard shove, she pushed George over the side. He was sent spiraling into the lagoon below. Zoey turned and marched into the cabin. She felt empowered yet there was an inkling that she just made things worse.

“So, I take it we’re staying?” Neil grumbled.

“I’ve waited years for this!” Tina exclaimed.

Mark was surprised at how much he fought off the urge to finish. Looking at her was like looking at a model in a magazine come to life. She shuddered several times between her thighs, involuntarily orgasming. Yet he continued to thrust into her.

Then they heard the shouting.

"What was that?" He tried to look over his shoulder, but Tina carefully placed a hand on his cheek and pulled him back to her.

"Don't stop!" Tina urged him. "Please."

George surfaced and quickly made his way to the ladder. When he began to ascend, there was a calming sensation that came over him. It was as if the water had an effect on him. He was not as furious as he normally would have been. Still, he was mad. He hopped on deck and made his way for the cabin.

Zoey sat there, hands in face. She looked as though she was crying.

"Listen here!" he began but stopped.

It was obvious now. She was not crying. She was laughing. He could not believe it. Her grin was astonishingly wide. There seemed to be a lot of build up behind it. As if she had waited for this moment for a decade.

He quickly raised his hand and slapped her across the face.

Neil heard the slap. It was so loud that he figured Cecilia and Leon heard it too. Then there were clattering noises. Stuff was being thrown around in there.

"What ever you break, you replace!" he called over his shoulder.

He looked out and saw the African American couple and began to mumble racial slurs. They were far enough away to not hear them.

Something close by did. Though it did not care for whatever came out of his mouth. It only wanted his insides.

The boat suddenly lurched to the starboard side. George was flung atop of Zoey. She tried to push him off, at first presuming it was another attack. Then she saw he was confused.

Eventually, he got up. "What the hell was that?"

Small plopping sounds could be heard on the roof. It spread across as if it were a wall of noise.

"Rain?" She screamed and then turned to look out the porthole behind her. "How could this day get any worse?"

The droplets were not clear. Rather they were red. Small, ruby-colored liquid that zigzagged down the glass.

"What the hell?"

Something wet and hard slapped against the window. She jumped back. The mangled face was mutilated almost to the point where she couldn't tell who it was. Then she noticed the beard.

"Neil!" she screamed in utter fright. Her hands curled as they shot to her face, covering her mouth.

George turned and saw him too. His body began to slide down. Only it stopped halfway. He had no waist or legs.

"Oh my god!" George cried out.

"Ahhh! What the fuck is that thing?" Cecilia screamed.

The creature was unlike anything any of them had seen before. It was long, scaly, yet had a misshapen head and spikes at the end of its tail. Its red eyes bore down on them. The little black slits were narrowing in on their location. It let out a hideous shriek as if to mock Cecilia's. The captain's legs fell out of its jaws and into the water below. Then, it lurched over and dove into the lagoon.

"Everyone get back to the boat!" Leon called out.

His powerful arms brought him towards the watercraft quickly. He looked behind him and saw that Cecilia was still there, frozen with fear. He turned back and made his way over.

As he did, he strained his head above the water. "Mark! Tina! C'mon, guys! We have to go now!"

This time, Tina looked around the log. She saw Leon grabbing Cecilia by the shoulder and dragging her towards the boat.

"What's going on now?" Mark asked, his manhood going slightly limp.

"I don't know. They seem scared though."

"It's probably a gator." Mark carefully pulled her off of him. "Let's get back to the boat. We'll pick this up later."

She leaned forward and kissed his cheek. "We'd better."

They both began to make their way over, their arms and legs casually pushing through the water. Side by side, they both stopped when Leon called back to them.

"Hurry up! It killed the captain!"

"What?" Tina asked, shocked.

"It's in the water! Come on!" Cecilia cried out.

"What's in the water?" Mark inquired.

They did not answer. Leon just brought Cecilia towards the stern.

"Get to the ladder!"

She began to ascend but not on the ladder. Her body rose higher and higher into the air. The jaws of the creature bit down on her midsection. Her guts shredded apart as it shook her back and forth. She managed to get out a blood curdling scream before she was dragged back down into the depths.

George walked out just as she went under. The water was clear and he could see the creature dragging her around like a ragdoll. Then, it consumed her with a couple of gulps. One of her legs still stuck out of its jaws. It bit down, snapping it like a twig.

"Nope!" He ran towards the ladder that led to the upper deck.

"What's happening?" Zoey asked, mid-sob.

"Don't come out here!" George shouted.

She had had enough of him telling her what to do and came out from below. She saw Mark and Tina were still a ways out. "What are you guys doing? Come on!"

Mark snapped out of it and grabbed Tina. The two then swam towards the boat. Their movements signified a frenzied response. Something terrible had happened alright.

Zoey ran towards the ladder to give them a hand. Leon's shot up first. She grabbed it and he climbed aboard.

"Where's Cecilia?"

Leon ignored her at first. He just plopped onto the deck and put his hands on his face.

"Where is she?"

"It got her!"

"What did? What's out there?" Zoey was losing patience. After seeing the captain's corpse fall, she wanted to know what was going on.

There was a splashing sound, and she turned to see Mark and Tina rushing towards the ladder. She turned to Leon.

"Help me get them aboard!"

Suddenly, the engine came to life.

"Wait! We need to get Mark and Tina out."

George looked over his shoulder. He saw Tina was already a few steps up the ladder. *Fuck you, Mark.*

He pushed the throttle forward and the cabin cruiser motioned away. Tina was not expecting it and she lost her grip, toppling into the water.

"Hey!" Mark screamed, angrily.

"What gives, man! Go back!" Leon shouted.

Looking down, George saw the creature. It was charging for Tina. "It's too late."

Leon and Zoey watched as the creature passed by the boat. Water brushed against its scales and its girth came further and further up on the surface.

Tina's jaw dropped as the large animal barreled towards her.

"No!" Mark screamed.

The massive jaws widened as it was practically atop her. She screamed so loud that it hurt Mark's ears. He could not turn away though. He began to swim towards her.

Impact. A single dart flew across the lagoon and imbedded itself in the roof of the creature's mouth. The stinging pain caused it to dive down, right past Tina.

"Get out of the water, now!" a voice called out to them.

At first, Mark was surprised he managed to reach Tina and wrap his arm around her waist. Then, when he pulled her away, he realized the creature was not after them anymore. The cabin cruiser was close to the entrance of the lagoon. He dragged her away.

"Let's go!"

"Where?" Her initial shock was wearing off.

"We have to get to that stump again. We have to hide!"

Tina's legs felt like cement blocks, but she managed to propel herself forward. Making their way across the lagoon was frightening enough, what with that monstrosity below. She reached for the log and began to climb but turned to look down. It was there again, about fifteen yards out.

"Don't stop!" he commanded.

She reached down. "Come with me!"

Mark grabbed hold and she pulled him close. She then continued up. The further she went, the more rotted it became.

"I'm losing my grip!"

He pressed against her legs to help her stay in place.

Before breaching the surface, it could be seen below. The outline was clear as day as were its scales and angry red eyes. It came up, rows upon rows of teeth glistening in the sunlight.

Another shot rang out. This time, it struck the creature in the gums. It roared in pain. Then, it began to move around awkwardly as if it were wobbling. Spasms shook through its whole body. It came forward, falling down onto the stump. Mark and Tina let go and landed in the water with a resounding splash.

Mark surfaced first. He spotted Tina on her back. "Hey!" he called out to her.

Swimming over with a brisk pace, he managed to hold her up. Her eyes parted slowly.

"Are you alright?" she asked.

He chuckled and then looked down at his intact manhood. "All good on this end. You?"

She smirked. "I'll live. I grew up around here."

He leaned forward and they kissed.

CHAPTER ELEVEN

Silent yet aware.

Whether the sedatives would last long or not, it was time to move the creature. Fred was currently hip deep in swamp water as Joe secured a rope to a tree on the shoreline. Both were on edge. They seemed to not know how much of the injection went in. Hence why they moved with such haste. Fred scolded his son for every mistake he made. Even if it was not that big of a deal.

Mark and Tina were back on the cabin cruiser, the former happy to finally put on his underwear. Tina did not hide the fact that she was watching him the whole time. She looked past his privates and was seeing the man as if she had just seen him for the first time. He did not give up on her. In fact, he tried to save her.

George, meanwhile, sulked below. He did not speak a word after the propellors got caught in some weeds. Leon and Zoey were down by the prop, attempting to unclog it. It was a slow-going process but it had to be done.

Joe turned and looked at the group. He noticed how shaken they were, yet they were still working together. Well, most of them. It was admirable. He turned to his father who was tossing the rope around the creature's girth for the umpteenth time. He wouldn't ask for his help on this if his life depended on it. If, by some odd chance, he did, he would just belittle him every step of the way.

"There we go." Fred secured a knot around it. "That should hold."

He then waded back to shore. Joe held out his hand to help his father but he slapped it away, ignoring him entirely.

"Alright, lets pull this sucker out of there," he ordered.

"It's not going to work," Joe stated.

"What do you mean, kid?"

"I mean that this is the biggest tree around, it won't be enough to bring it in. The rope will cut right through it after a few minutes."

"It'll only take a few minutes to tow that big ol' bitch in! Use your head!" Fred lambasted his son.

Begrudgingly, Joe began to go forward, rope in hand. Fred grabbed another section of it and followed.

"Hey, big guy!" he shouted at Leon. "Wanna come help us out here?"

Leon looked up but did not answer. His eyes were red and puffy. Still, they bore into Fred's own with disdain.

"Suit yourself."

The two hunters continued out. Stepping into the lagoon, Joe immediately snapped into uneasiness. They were coming up on the creature's tail. He had seen the aftermath of that guy in the car and the blood-splattered remains of whomever was on that speedboat. They looked like they had exploded. Joe had a feeling it had to do with those spikes. They were long, thick, and a sickly brownish yellow. There was something about them. He wondered if they were poisonous.

"What exactly did they combine?"

"Huh?" Fred looked at him.

"Well, you said we were going hybrid hunting. I was just wondering what this thing actually is."

Fred, at first, did not want to say anything. Focusing on the obstacle at hand was far more important. He noticed how on-edge his son was though and thought it would help ease his mind. Or, at the very least, distract him from terrible thoughts.

"Eeligator."

"What?"

"It's an eeligator. Part eel, part alligator. You've seen those spikes on its tail. They conduct a shit ton of electrical currents that can zap its prey. I've seen it blow up a cow one time with the sheer amount of charge the current brought."

"Why does it only have two feet on the front?"

"A genetic fuck up. The scientists figured it could use them to help with speed and maneuverability. If you ask me, it just makes it look goofier."

They were soon passing by its midsection.

"So, what do I do if it wakes up?"

"Pray."

"I'm being serious."

"Me too," Fred said coldly.

"You're willing to put me in front of that thing before yourself?"

Fred did not answer.

"Just when I thought you couldn't stoop any lower."

"Let's just finish this."

Joe stopped in his tracks. "I'm not so sure I want to."

"This isn't a game, son."

"Oh, so now I'm your son?"

"Of course you are. What is this? Fifty questions?"

"I've only got one for you." Joe turned to face his father. "Do you hate me?"

Putting his palm on his forehead, Fred brought his hand down over his entire face. "You need to understand something. I'm not the kind of guy you want to like you."

"You're still my father."

"Yeah, and I'm a father with a past darker and shadier than some politicians."

"I don't care. You're still my dad."

Fred stood there, dumbstruck as his son turned his back to him and continued to pull the rope. He eventually managed to grab hold as well, but he was not picking up the slack.

"Hurry up. I don't want to be out here all day," Joe shouted at him.

They were at the head now. The jaws were barely parted.

"Let me go up front," Fred said.

"I've got it," Joe sneered. "I wouldn't want it to come for me while I wasn't looking now, would I?"

Passing by the creature entirely, they soon heard its scaly body rubbing against the shore. The line was getting noticeably harder to pull now that the creature was out of the water.

"C'mon, pull!" Fred ordered, gritting his teeth.

Joe looked over his shoulder and saw the eeligator's body was only a quarter of the way onto the shore. It was still asleep. For now.

"I'm trying!" he shouted.

Neither man had much energy left by the time they reached the halfway point.

"This isn't going to work!" Joe snapped at his dad.

Before Fred could answer, a guttural, groaning sound could be heard. They both turned and saw the cabin cruiser's engine had started.

"Now will you help us?" Fred called out to Leon.

He did not answer.

Zoey walked over towards the stern. "Why should we?"

"We need to get this animal ashore. It's the only way we can secure it for extraction."

"Not our problem." Leon came over, standing next to Zoey.

"Oh, so, if this fails, and more people die, it won't be your fault?" Fred made a show of his overexaggerated hand gestures as he spoke.

"It's not our fault that thing's out here," Mark added.

"No, but you're all a part of this now. Whether you like it or not."

"Bullshit," Leon laughed. "This isn't our mission, bro."

"Just get this thing ashore and we'll never have to work together again. I promise." Fred smiled.

"No!" Leon shouted.

"Wait," Zoey said. "What if it gets free?"

"Not our problem, Zo'." Leon turned to her.

"It will be if it chases us. I don't know about you, but I won't sleep well at night knowing that thing killed people, and we could have stopped it," Zoey explained.

Leon pondered for a moment and then turned to the two hunters. "Give us the rope."

The swamp had suddenly fallen silent. Eerie, unknown, the whole area had been alive with sounds but had slipped into a kind of cosmic void. One where there was no life, only noise. It was not visible, yet it could be heard.

Fred noticed it right away. There was something off. It had to be the creature being ashore now. There was no other explanation. A faint gust of warm wind blew by, causing a chill to run up his spine. He could not fathom why. It was anything but cold out.

Joe noticed the absence of sound then. It was out of the ordinary, sure. The job ahead required concentration though. The surroundings were the least of his concern. He continued to secure the line to the transom. Leon had given it a shot but failed each time.

George was still below but managed to throw his opinions on the matter out. *We should just leave it. Why not kill it?* The latter caused Fred to turn on him, shouting that he didn't know what was at stake.

"Alright, it's all set," Joe said as he stood up straight.

"We could use your help now, Mr. Barkley," Fred called out.

George begrudgingly left the cabin. His brooding demeanor remained but he still did what he was told. He was clearly humiliated every step of the way. Zoey took great joy out of that.

As he made his way up the ladder he looked back. The creature was still halfway in the water. "How far am I supposed to tow this sucker?"

"Until it's all the way ashore," Fred explained.

"We should go down below," Tina told Mark.

"Why?"

"What are we contributing here except being in the way?"

He pondered briefly. "I guess we can."

They made their way into the cabin just as George turned the key in the ignition. "Away we go."

The engine roared to life. He then pushed the throttle forward. Everyone on the deck watched as the scaly serpent came up out of the water like some lost treasure found in the bog. Suctioning sounds and water displacement filled the area. It had a muddy odor to it.

"Let's make this quick," Zoey stated. "Damn thing stinks."

"I don't think it'll take too much longer," Joe explained as the head began to emerge from the lagoon. First the backside came up. The scales were black and covered in muck. The aroma was disgusting. Following that, the back of its jaws became visible, as did those horrid teeth.

Fred looked at it. "Ugly fucker."

"Yep," Joe concurred. He then placed his foot on the stern and leaned forward. "Does it always sleep with its eyes open?"

"I'm afraid." Tina was leaning against Mark.

"Don't be. I won't let anything happen to you." He kissed the top of her head.

"I can't even think of what that thing is capable of. Why would someone make such a thing?"

"Money. Warfare. Who knows?"

She snuggled against him.

He felt stirring in his underwear. "Oh, God. I'm going to miss you when you leave."

"Why don't you come back with me?"

"Back where? You always move around. I don't really like moving around too much. I grew up here."

"So did I," she stated and then remained silent for a brief time. "I'll stay with you."

"What?"

"I have enough money to get by."

"I couldn't hold you back like that."

"I've wanted you ever since Sophomore year. Now that I finally have you, I don't want to lose you."

He smirked. "I'm glad you like dogs. I'm sure mine will love you."

"Aw. Boy or girl?"

"Boy."

"What's his name?"

"Buster."

"Adorable." She inched forward and planted a kiss on his cheek. He looked away sheepishly. "Just like you."

He laughed.

"It's alive!" they heard Zoey scream outside.

Mark quickly went into protection mode. "Stay here."

"No! Let's just hide."

"I can't do that. They may need my help."

"I'll come too," Tina told him.

"Please. I don't want anything to happen to you." He looked back at her. Her face was flushed with fear. "I won't leave the cabin. I just want to see outside."

She nodded, tears welling up in her eyes. "Be careful."

Mark continued towards the door. He felt the gravity of the situation was placed on his shoulders. There was no telling exactly what was going on. Had the creature swum off? He heard no commotion on the deck. Perhaps they were watching it make its way out of the lagoon.

He poked his head out and saw that everyone was still rigid with fear. They possessed a calm about them that Mark had not suspected. Then he saw why.

The creature was there. It was staring them down. Its eyes bore into his, locked in a hypnotic contest of ability. Mark was afraid to even blink. He began to find it difficult to stand as well. It seemingly possessed his muscles and weakened him to his bones.

"What do we do?" he heard Leon ask.

"We wait," Fred stated.

"Wait for what? For that big sucka to eat us?" Leon whispered sharply through barely parted lips.

Without warning, it slipped into the water. It left behind a small splash and rings of ripples.

"Oh, thank God," Zoey exhaled.

"Don't count your blessings," Fred said coldly.

A shift in the atmosphere made Mark feel a calm wash over him. It had been like he locked eyes with the devil and won. He went back into the cabin.

"Is it gone?" Tina asked.

"Yes. I think it's gone," Mark said softly.

There was a sense of peace that turned into chaos when the cabin cruiser rocked on its portside.

"Holy shit!" they heard George scream.

"Get up here!" Zoey called down to them.

Mark grabbed Tina's hand tightly and the two ran to the exit. Behind them, they could hear shattered fiberglass and splintered wood. It had broken through the hull.

"Hurry!" Zoey cried.

They both came out as the creature broke in. Fred aimed at the tranquilizer and was preparing to fire. It would have to be a direct hit. Not on the body, the scales were too tough. He took a deep breath and aimed for its open mouth as it charged out from below. It tried to get through the doorway but was having trouble. As it fidgeted, it snapped its jaws around wildly.

"Back it up!" Fred shouted at the group.

As the maniacal creature's jaws widened and then slammed shut, its head turned and nearly chomped down on Tina's long legs. Mark quickly scooped her up and held her close.

"Shoot it!" Mark screamed.

Joe reached for the blade tucked into his belt. Something had to be done, and his father was taking too long. He unsheathed it and charged for the beast.

"Kid! No!" Fred's eyes widened in alarm.

With one long bounding jump, Joe leapt atop the animal. It shook back and forth, up and down, but he held on. He then raised his hand holding the knife. It was almost as long as a machete and appeared sharper. He drove it down. Metal met scale and the metal lost. The blade snapped with a loud tinging noise.

"Joe!" Fred raised his gun again.

The creature then bucked up and down. Joe was flung around wildly. He had ridden hogs when he was a boy, but this was several species higher than that. A horse or bull would cower in fear at the very sight of this thing. Suddenly, he was sent soaring through the air. He landed hard on the deck, not far from the gaping jaws.

A sudden rush of water began to fill the deck.

"Abandon ship!" Leon ordered.

"You don't have to tell me twice!" George quickly hopped off and into the lagoon.

Fred ran towards Joe. The bow was dipping now, the pulpit practically touching the water. He grabbed his son around the collar and hoisted him up just as the jaws snapped where he once lay.

"Don't ever do something that stupid again!" Fred snapped at him.

Joe gave him a blank stare.

"Let's go!" He pushed his son into the water without any warning.

He then followed him. Everyone else was already near the shore. The creature let out a roar so mighty that some of the windows shattered in the cabin. It was not clear if it was because the boat was crumbling apart or that the creature's vocals were that powerful.

With Fred and Joe now ashore, the group began to trudge through the muddy landscape. Zoey turned back and saw the oversized animal was splitting the boat apart. It eventually collapsed atop it, sinking below.

"Did that kill it?" she wondered.

Mark walked over. "I don't think so."

He placed a hand on her shoulder. "C'mon. Let's get the hell out of here."

Tina watched as they made their way over to the group. She tried not to feel upset. They were all friends stuck in a horrible situation. It was not the time for petty emotions to get in the way. Still, she wondered.

CHAPTER TWELVE

Pushing through.

The cabin cruiser had cracked over its massive head. Besides an irritating headache, the creature was unharmed. Momentarily stunned, it came around after a few minutes and began to break through the debris, snapping at fallen pieces of wood and batting fiberglass chunks with its girthy cranium. There had been a lot of energy used during its recent attack and escape. Now it needed to be satiated.

There was not a long passage of time from when it broke the surface until it reached the shore. An overwhelming scent filled its nostrils. The smell of its prey. They were making their way through the swamp. It sniffed the air and pinpointed which direction they were heading.

It was different now though. This was personal. They had tried to destroy it. Things would be handled with more cunning from now on. It would not be so careless and voracious. There would be methods applied.

A hunt would begin.

Slithering towards the direction of the bodily meat sacks, it did not take long to find them. They had not made it far from shore. Its vision saw the brush being pushed first. Yellow and green formed outlines around red shapes. They were quickly spotted and yet it held back. They were seven, it was one. Even still, it had the advantage. Biding its time, it kept its distance.

***

"It's getting close to starting time!" a middle-aged woman shouted.

The crew of the Wyman High School Reunion consisted of two waiters, a chef and his three cooks, as well as a DJ. The rest of the personnel were teachers and some of the students that offered to stay after school and help with the displays and getting everything ready.

Mrs. Ronald made her way over to her husband. "It's coming along."

"I think we'll be ready in time." He smiled warmly at her.

"Did you hear from Zoey Francis yet?"

"Not a peep since this morning."

"Well, I hope they make it here safe and on time." She then added, "She was a great student."

"2015 was one of the last good classes," Mr. Ronald chuckled.

A student walked by behind them. She had her black hair in a tight bun and had red rimmed glasses.

"I heard that!" she said louder than she probably meant, seemingly hurt by the statement.

"Well, Wendy. When do we let them in?" Mr. Ronald asked his wife.

"In half an hour. I want to make sure everything is perfect."

"Okie dokie," he laughed.

She giggled in response. "You sound like a middle school girl when you say that, Bud."

"At least I don't say it that often."

Both made their way towards the tables where the rest of the teachers were sitting.

Mr. Powers stood at the end of one of the tables. He was shouting commands. In his older age, he was becoming cranky and crotchety. The younger generation could not stand him.

Wendy reluctantly approached him. “We’re almost all set up at the tables.”

“Hmm? Oh. Yes. Well, I still think there needs to be more chairs.”

“It’s not a wedding, Principal Powers. There won’t be more than twenty people who show up if I were to guess.”

“You would know all about weddings, Mrs. Ronald.”

“Yes, well. Fraternizing between staff being off the table was a dumb rule to begin with.” She spun on her heels and walked along the table to assist any of the students.

The principal grumbled. “Let’s make sure the forks and spoons are on the left side, shall we?”

***

“Can we stop!” George shouted. “I need a break!”

“That thing will catch up if we do!” Tina said, fear covering her tone.

“It already has,” Fred said as he took a seat on a nearby rock.

“What do you mean?” Mark took a step towards him.

“It’s been hunting us this whole time.”

“I haven’t heard anything.”

“It’s far enough away. Don’t worry though. It sees us.”

“This is ridiculous!” George shouted.

“Take a chill pill, man,” Leon said. “You’re going to draw it right to us!”

"Haven't you listened to a word Crocodile Dundee has said?" George spat. "It already knows where we are."

"We have to keep our heads if we want to stay alive," Mark stated.

"Shut the fuck up, Stanton! You're not helping anything but yourself!" George screamed at the man.

"What are you talking about?" Mark wondered, genuinely confused.

"You know *exactly* what I'm saying!" He jabbed a finger into his chest. "You think you're hot shit! Always have! I'll tell you one thing. If you even give my woman puppy eyes, it'll be your biggest mistake."

Mark slowly brushed George's appendage from him and smiled. "Don't act like you are some kind of saint."

"What?" George was taken aback.

"You think we can't see the pounds of makeup applied to certain parts of her face. When's the last time you hit her, huh? It couldn't have been that long ago? Probably back on the boat, perhaps?"

George tried to size him up. Mark did not back down.

"Guys, stop! This is getting ridiculous!" Zoey walked over.

"Stay out of this, bitch!" George snapped at her.

"This isn't helping matters," Leon tried to be the voice of reason.

"Get this, Stanton!" George stared down at Mark. "You're six-foot nothing. Emphasis on nothing. I will clobber you."

"Then do it." Mark stood his ground.

Tina watched helplessly "Please don't hurt each other. We need to work together to get out of here!"

"Ha!" George laughed heartily. "The only things working for you are your career and those jugs on your chest. You left us high and dry out in the swamps for fame and glory."

"I don't owe anyone here anything," Tina stated.

"Give it up, Barkley!" Mark told him. "You're not fooling anyone."

Clenching his fists hard as he gritted his teeth, George tried to ignore the concerns. He wanted to clobber Mark into a pulp. He was bigger, stronger, but slower and fatter. There was no guarantee he would win. Instead, he spat on the ground next to him and waved him off.

"Maybe next time then?" Mark chuckled.

No one spoke for a whole minute. The silence caused Joe's anxiety to bloom.

"We should get going," he stated. "It's going to get dark soon."

"So much for our reunion," Zoey said.

Fred stood up. "That creature got a better one."

"What do you mean?" Leon asked.

"That thing, it belonged here at one point." He pointed over his shoulder. "Yep. Right out there in the swamp. It's a creature of nature alright."

"Bull. I've never seen anything like that out here," Mark stated.

"It was at one point. Now it's different," Fred explained. "Ah, the less you know the better."

He began to trudge through some muck when Mark placed a hand on his shoulder.

"What is it?"

Fred turned and faced him. "Take your hand off me. Unlike your friend over there, I'm not afraid to throw down."

George looked down at himself.

Mark relinquished his grip. "What are we dealing with?"

"It's not my problem." Fred then sighed. "Trust me. You don't want to know any more than I've already told you."

For some reason unfathomable to Mark, he believed this man. There were likely dark dealings going on with this creature. The less he knew, the better. As far as he was concerned, his priority was to get everyone to safety. He made no notion of being the leader, but he was the most level headed next to these two hunters. He was going to step up whether George liked it or not.

***

Her patience was running low. After Trudy spent an hour going over the very simple equipment with Kathy, the woman had still seemed lost. It was growing darker by the minute. Nothing seemed to be processing in the grieving lady's head. Every time she asked if she were all set, she would give a sigh as if to ask if she could go over it again.

She did not leave the Wisner estate until six o' clock on the dot. It would be dark in two hours or so. If she wanted to make any progress, she had to start her search this evening. As she drove down the road, she noticed swamplands on either side of her.

"This is a hell of a place to live, Jordon." She spoke to him as if he were in the passenger seat next to her.

A garbled noise came over the radio.

"This is Fawn, repeat that. Is that you Wisner? Over."

"Yes, it's me. Just making sure I'm tuned into the right station."

"It's a frequency. Over."

"A what?"

"Never mind. Just say *over* when you're done. Over."

"Okay. Sorry. Over."

Trudy fished out a cigarette from her purse and lit it. She normally did not like smoking in cars, but this was a rental. Possessing enough curtesy to roll down the window, she reached for the button. The glass came down and she got her first whiff of the marshes. Her hand immediately covered her nose.

"Lord Almighty. I hope it doesn't smell this bad out there."

Reconsidering her kindly gesture, she rolled the window back up. The smoke fought off the muddy odor.

It was not much later she saw the caution tape hung up by two trees. She was thankful no squad or patrol cars were there. No one was on guard. The investigation was pending but there were doubts he was still in there. The tape was more so to keep people out in case there was a potential crime scene.

She parked her car on the bright green grass. The vehicle lurched forward a bit when her foot released the brake. She could tell the wheels were already sinking in the mud a bit.

"Next time I'll opt for a jeep."

Already sporting a pair of muck boots and slacks, she got out and made her way over towards the taped off area. Lifting it, she felt a sudden chill run down her back. Bending over, she fought the urge to turn back and was now on the other side.

"Let's do this."

CHAPTER THIRTEEN

Molding the empire.

Disappearing behind a throng of trees, the sun dipped beyond the horizon, plunging the swamp into blackness. The moon was not far behind but was slowly casting its gloomy hue to naturally light the woods. Crickets stridulated but other insects seemed to come out as well. Mosquitoes were in full force and spiders crawled along the muddy forest floor. Frog croaking intensified and random splashes could be heard as small fish breached the surface to snatch a nighttime snack.

The absence of light was making everyone turn to Fred who carried one by his side. It was not on. Even his son seemed to gaze at him every so often. It was as if he were trying to annoy or guilt him into pressing the bubbly button atop it. Casting light was a last resort in his father's mind though.

No one wanted to bring up the very real fact that it already knew where they were. Fred seemed agitated and there was no need to progress their guide's temper further. Still, they needed a source of light and fast.

"Let's have it," George said suddenly.

"Fuck off," Fred said sourly.

"We need light, Dad," Joe stated.

"We'll be fine. I know where we are."

"We've been walking in circles," Zoey said.

"How would you know that?" Fred laughed.

"Because I can still hear the swamp. We're nowhere near the road, are we?"

A sudden beam was cast in Zoey's direction. He stared at her with his deep, sullen eyes and repeated, "I know where we are."

"Let me see that!" Mark made an attempt to snatch the flashlight from the man's hand. He was only successful in grabbing hold of it. Unable to pry it from his hands, he gave it a few hard yanks.

"Give it up."

"We need light!" Joe shouted.

"Get a grip, boy. Don't turn against me."

"I'm not. We just need to see where we're going. Even I don't know where we are."

"Wait!" Leon said suddenly.

"What?" Tina shuddered in fright. She inched closer to Zoey.

"Do you smell that?"

"Smell what?" Joe asked.

Leon took a step closer towards some thickets. "It smells like smoke."

"Kathy. Do you read me? Over?" Trudy repeated for the umpteenth time.

She was on her eighth cigarette since she wandered out into the swamp. The area began to eat at her like the incessant mosquitoes. Her temper could only be controlled by nicotine so much.

"Jesus Christ, Kathy. Please answer me. Over."

No response.

She then heard a twig snap and saw a light turn on.

"Shit! Cops!" she whispered to herself.

Hunching over, sitting on her knees now, she watched as the light danced around through the trees. There was a clear sign of distress in the illuminated agitation. Some scenarios ran through her mind. *What if they're hurt? Or what if they are hurting someone? Did they find the perpetrator in Jordon's disappearance? Were they hurting Jordon for disappearing? Why would they? Unless they were mad.*

Either way, she had to help him. If not for Kathy's sake, then for her own. A plume of smoke escaped her barely parted lips, and she headed towards the light.

"I think someone's coming," Leon said.

Joe raised his gun. "Someone or something?"

"I can't tell. Fred, shine your light over there."

"I will once this wannabe Rambo lets go of it."

Mark relinquished the flashlight immediately. Fred then shone it over where Leon was. There was some rustling in the bushes ahead of him.

"C'mon out," Leon said calmly.

A woman with crazed, tussled hair and smeared lipstick came charging out. An anger burned in her eyes like that of an animal on the hunt. Leon caught her mid stride.

"Who the hell are you people?" she screamed.

"Why don't you start?" Fred asked.

She wiggled her way out of Leon's muscular grip and composed herself. "My name is Trudy Fawn. I'm looking for someone."

"It's too late, Trudy," a familiar voice came over the radio.

"Who's that?" Joe asked, still pointing his gun at her.

"Oh, thank God. Kathy. Can you hear me?"

"I could hear you this whole time."

"I've been trying to get ahold of you."

"I know."

"Then why didn't you say anything?"

"Because you were supposed to die an hour ago."

"Wait? What?"

"Mrs. Wisner?" Fred asked, genuinely surprised. "Aw, I thought I recognized your nasally voice."

"You know her?" Trudy turned to him in shock.

"Not personally, no. She's a secretary at Mr. Boudreaux's office."

"Regardless of who I really am, the mission must be carried out."

"What about your husband?" Trudy asked.

"I know about you two," Kathy continued without missing a beat. *"He's a piece of shit figuratively and literally. His steaming pile was picked up by our camera feeds earlier this morning."*

"You have camera feeds?" Joe wondered.

Trudy paid no mind to that, instead, focusing on the obvious. "No way. Jordon can't be dead!"

"Yes, deary. He was killed the day he went missing. The men who are there with you that work for Boudreaux, they saw to that."

"Not true. The thing escaped," Jordon stated. "It was a complete accident."

"No problem. We still need you to catch the experiment and get it back to the lab in one piece."

Fred looked from Trudy to Joe. "Consider it done. Just let Boudreaux know it's killed at least two more people."

"Duly noted." There was a click as Kathy went offline.

Trudy stood there, baffled. "I can't believe it."

"Oh, you'd better believe it," Fred said. "We should probably get moving."

"Wait!" Mark took a step towards him. "Is that why we're still deep in the swamp? So, you can finish your mission."

"You don't understand."

"Yes, I do!" Mark shouted. "It just killed two people. One of which was a good friend. We want out of here, pronto!"

"I think the body count is up to five or six now actually, but that's beside the point."

"You're sick."

"…And you're being hunted. We all are. If we try to get closer to the road, we'll end up chow," Fred continued. "At least if we stay, we'll have a fighting chance."

"How many bullets you got left?" Leon asked Joe.

"One tranquilizer dart. The pistol's chamber is full."

"And you, Mr. Dundee?"

"Me? I've got a knife. Don't worry though. It won't run out of bullets."

"I don't believe this!" Tina looked around, scared.

Mark made his way over and placed a hand on her shoulder.

"So, what do you suggest?"

Fred sighed. "I suggest we quit the small talk. It's going to be a long night."

Every minute seemed like an eternity when walking through nature. It was as if time slowed for a brief period where one could be in isolation and either enjoy or loathe every breathtaking moment. The constant search for one's inner self was a crusade many did not accomplish. It proved to be day-to-day distractions that kept individuals from achieving their peace. The search was as long as they kept resisting.

Fred was the only one amongst them that had accomplished this goal. When Mrs. Brady had been pregnant with Joe, he had run off. He was not ready. The unplanned parent had trudged off deep into the woods and eventually came back a new man. He had changed and not for the betterment of his family. Rather for himself.

Joe had become rebellious while Fred's attachment grew further from his wife and son's. Now the two men were in the swamps of Florida trekking after a monster. Joe was a halfway decent tracker; Fred would give him that. He did not know squat when it came to aiming and pulling the trigger though. Especially the former.

"It was just another gig," Joe said suddenly.

He was standing by Fred's side, a look of shame appearing on his face. It was as if he thought he had been caught doing something wrong. This time it was the latter that was correct. They had not been made yet.

"What are you on about?"

"People are dying. How many more have to in order for you to call it quits?" Joe asked.

"I'm tired of having to explain myself to you. There is no justification for what I've done and I'm content with that. Why can't you be?"

Joe continued on in silence.

There was not much chatter behind them. Zoey occasionally glared at George as he fought himself not to give in and look back. Leon was practically unresponsive. Seeing Cecilia torn apart before his very eyes scarred him deeply. Trudy brought up the rear with her flashlight scanning the trees behind them and occasionally trying to get a call out to the police.

"They must have jammed my phone somehow. Does anyone else have a cell?"

"Ours sank into the everglades along with the boat," Zoey stated.

Trudy turned to the hunters. "What about you two?"

"They did the same to ours even before we were enroute to drop off the specimen," Fred explained.

She did not press further. It was pointless to do so. They needed to save their energy to survive.

Mark and Tina held hands as they walked. Both were dressed down to the nitty gritty. Mark with his whites and nothing else, Tina with her metallic green halter bikini. Inwardly, they were thankful it was not cold. There was just enough chill to not attract too many insects to them. Part of Mark hoped they were going after George relentlessly.

"I've missed you," Tina said softly.

Mark partially turned to her. "I can't remember the last time I've been this happy with someone."

"It's been a long time coming," she whispered into his ear.

"Let's focus, people," Fred called back over his shoulder.

A manmade bridge, created by rope and logs, lay before them. They were near a stream. The babbling water was peaceful to listen to.

"Alright," Fred began. "I'll cross first. I'll figure out how many it can hold. Then we'll go from there."

He was careful at first. Making sure the lashing was secure and held together tightly, the first few steps were worrisome. After a few more steps, he was content. The bridge was only five feet or so in length and the water below couldn't be any deeper than a foot. It was enough to slow their progress though.

"I think it can hold two at a time. Preferably side by side near the center."

Leon backed over to Trudy who was slipping her flashlight in her back pocket. "George, you and Zoey go first. Mark and Tina next. I'll cross with Trudy."

"You don't have to tell me twice," George chuckled.

Zoey made her way towards the edge. She looked down at the logs. "Are they slippery?"

“No,” Fred said flatly.

“Give me your hand.” Geroge held out his own.

She did not oblige. Instead, she took a step onto the makeshift bridge. George quickly hopped up after her. They both hurried across.

“We haven’t got all day here, folks,” Fred stated.

Joe was next and his father knew it. He had not even been given the chance to take a step forward before he made that comment. It ate at him, his skin crawling at the very thought of his words.

He then looked back at Mark and Tina. “You two next. I’ll bring up the rear.”

“You afraid, boy?” Fred laughed.

“No. I just want to make sure everyone is safe.”

“Mhm?”

Mark and Tina, hands interlocked tightly, quickly found their way across the bridge. Leon and Trudy were next.

“You guys go. I’ll make sure nothing happens,” Joe said.

“Just be careful. I don’t like this,” Leon explained,

A step onto one of the logs made a cracking sound. Or so they thought. Something was making its way through the brush.

“Hurry!” Joe shouted.

“Go!” Leon pushed Trudy.

One step in and her foot twisted in the grooves between the logs. “Ah shit!”

“Help her!” Tina cried out.

Joe and Leon ran to her aid.

“Let’s go! C’mon!” both men spoke in unison as they hefted her off the ground.

It came slithering out of the darkness like a dragon exiting its lair. The closer it got, the more the flashlight shone against its hide.

“Ahhh!” Tina screamed in horror.

The size of the creature seemed to grow by the way the torchlight danced off its scale-laden skin.

"Run!" Fred screamed.

Everyone hurried in a straight line, only maneuvering differently when confronted with obstacles like trees and thick brush.

"Let's go!" Leon said as he and Joe carried Trudy.

Their pace was slow. The creature somehow took note of this and slithered around them. It was as if it wanted to give those who thought they had a chance no salvation.

"Goddamnit!" Joe cried out.

"Go! Save them!" Trudy said.

"Are you sure?" He turned to Leon.

"I've got this," he replied.

After unslinging her arm from around his shoulder, Joe took off running into the night.

"I wish I had a cigarette right about now," Trudy groaned.

CHAPTER FOURTEEN

From bad to worse.

Lost. Tina had to admit what she feared most to herself. Everything was pitch black save for the moon that blanketed the canopies with its nightly glow. It glistened in its light rays that punched through a few of the trees with tremendous brilliance. If she were not so afraid, she would have wanted a selfie. There was no other way about it though. She was downright petrified.

No one else was nearby. She had lost Mark's grip somewhere shortly after the bridge. A very unsettling feeling crawled up her skin like a million spiders. She wanted to brush the metaphorical insects off but was trying to remain alert. The darkness played tricks on her. Every inky space of blackened voids shouted at her to stay away. If only she could see, it would be clear it was just shrubbery.

A soft patch graced her sore feet. She had no shoes on, having left her high heels on the now destroyed cabin cruiser. She was simply alone in a barbaric land. All that comforted her was the grass between her toes.

She thought back on the meditation she learned from the classes she took and began to breathe in through her nose and out her mouth. She repeated the process a few times, clearing her mind of the fear surrounding her. She was at ease by the time she heard the first cracking of sticks.

Quickly, she began to hyperventilate. She inwardly begged that it was Mark. Pleaded to any higher power that would listen. Her hands found their way to her face as she covered her mouth in clawing fright. She tried to say his name. Only a faint whimper emerged. With that soft call, the sticks began to break closer. Her lower lip trembled as the barely distinguishable shape of something large emerged through the low hanging vines. The signs of agitation and rage were prevalent.

"Oh no!"

"Mark?" Tina heard the shape talk.

"Tina?" The shape suddenly froze in place.

"Thank God!" She hurried over to him.

"Help. Get me out of here!"

She began to tear at the vines. "I thought it was that thing!"

"Hurry! That *thing* is right behind me!"

Tina froze momentarily. At first, Mark thought she was going to run off, abandoning him. It would not be the first time a woman did that. To his surprise, she continued pulling at the vines. Only now she was feverish in her attempt.

"I'll get you out of there!"

A guttural growl could be heard behind him. Mark was limp with defeat. "Tina. Go."

"What? No! I'm going to help you!" Tina managed to get a few more clumps off his wrist.

He lunged forward, practically slamming into her. "Go before it gets you too!"

Eyes now watering, Tina did not even get a chance to reconsider. Mark kicked at her wildly and she backed up. He looked at her ashamedly.

"I love you. I always have," Tina said and then turned and ran.

"I love you too!" he called after her.

A barrage of sounds echoed through the swamp behind him. He closed his eyes, awaiting the painful inevitable. The teeth bearing down on him, shredding him to pieces. He could practically feel the hot breath on his back. If he had indeed turned, the sight of the cavernous jaws would have been what greeted him.

The creature was inches from him when the first shot rang out. The tranquilizer dart hit right above its gums, on a scaly portion of its skin. It did little more than irritate it briefly.

Joe stood there momentarily. He quickly reached for the pistol, but it fumbled in his hands. The weapon hit the ground hard just as the creature's spikes hit him in his chest, penetrating through, cracking several ribs in the process. A blue glow began to emerge in the night. It was coming from the backside of the animal, as if it were charging up. All Joe could do was stand there, pinned in place, as an enormous electrical current surged through his body.

Mark turned in time to see the man's dead body dancing, contorting in unnatural directions. Then, before he could fully process what he was seeing, the hunter exploded into a crimson cloud of gore and meat chunks. He faced away as some sprayed onto his bare back.

Then he heard the scream. He turned and saw Tina standing there, paralyzed. Her bright red lips were parted as her mouth remained in an eternal howl of horror.

"I said run!" Mark cried out more so than commanded.

She could only manage to back up slowly, stepping on several clumps of dead leaves along the way. The crackling sound drew the creature to her location. Mark could only watch as it slithered past him. It did not occur to him that it was because he was still and she moving until it was too late.

The eeligator rose above her. Its jagged snaggleteeth were the stuff of nightmares. Red orbs were its eyes and the black slits in them were narrowed on her.

"Please," she begged softly.

Its head reared back.

"Ahhhhh!" she shrieked.

Closing down around her torso, the creature's bite was hard enough to tear through skin, flesh, and bone in one crush. Once it pulled up, it took her upper half with it. One of her pale arms dangled from its jaws. The other one severed at the shoulder and fell to the ground. Her legs did as well and innards uncoiled and spilled out of her midsection, onto the ground.

Mark did not say a word as the creature finished her off and made its way back into the black of night. He only looked in shock at the remains of his high school crush.

***

Fred could sense something was wrong. At the sight of Mark caught in the vines, remaining still, his first thought was that another one of his friends had been killed. It was never a pleasant thing, death. Still, he had a job to do. He took a step forward and stepped in something squishy.

The entire area around him was coated in red. It looked as though a giant rose had blossomed and then exploded, splattering red in every direction. He examined the sight before him. It was not pretty. Some poor sap had met a similar fate to those on that boat they found.

"Sorry about your friend here." Fred stood up and continued towards Mark.

"That's not my friend," he replied coldly.

Stopping in his tracks, the sudden realization of what he said came over him. His whole world began to spin, and dizziness slowly took over.

"No," he whispered.

"I'm sorry about your son," Mark added.

Taking a step back, he tried to steady himself. "What am I going to tell his mother?"

"Please. Sir. You have to help me get untangled. That thing could be back any moment," Mark explained.

The hunter was not paying any attention to the pleading man. His mind reeled from the thought of telling his bipolar wife that their son was nothing more than a stain in the grass. Dead was an understatement. The poor kid had been blown up as if he stepped on a landmine.

"I can't do this," Fred said softly.

"You need to help us!" Mark raised his voice slightly.

"I couldn't even help my own son."

"He died trying to save us."

"Us?"

Mark gulped. "It got Tina."

"Who?"

If Mark were free, he would slap the man. Maybe a jab to the face. It was not imperative that he knew the names of those he was trying to help keep alive. The way he said it got under his skin though.

"The one with the red hair."

"That's a damn shame," Fred said absentmindedly.

"Are you even listening to me? You need to help me!" Mark realized he had not been able to turn to face Fred this whole time. He was taken by surprise when the vines began to loosen. He cut at them with his trusty blade.

Falling to the ground below, Mark tried to get up but realized most of his strength was gone. It was not depleted though. *Is this what it feels like to give up?*

"Where is it now?" Fred asked.

Mark could barely lift his hand, but he managed to point ahead. "It went that way."

"Let's go."

"Why?" He looked up at the hunter, teary-eyed.

"We have to save what's left of your friends."

Pulling him to his feet, Fred gave Mark a once over. "You good?"

"Yes," he replied, unsure but eager.

"Did he leave any weapons behind?"

"I think he still had his pistol. I couldn't see him. I heard the tranquilizer dart fly by."

Fred quickly made his way over to the red spread that was what was left of his son. It did not take him long to find the weapon for it was right before the remains. He picked it up and examined it.

"Will it still fire?" Mark asked.

Going over and placing the pistol in Mark's hands, he tried to force a smile. It did little to reassure. "Don't miss."

"What about you?"

"I have my blade and a little going away present."

"What do you mean?" Mark asked.

"You'll know when the time comes." Fred patted him on the shoulder.

The two then hurried towards the direction the creature was last seen. It was not long before they heard its scaly body brushing against the swamp floor.

"How did we catch up to it so fast?" Mark wondered.

"It's hunting."

"How can you tell?"

"Because it's keeping its distance. We have to keep quiet if we're going to take it out."

Mark immediately went silent. The creature was there, clear as day under the moonlit night. The jagged teeth glistened in the rays as its red eyes seemed to glow in the dark. They narrowed on something. Or someone.

"Where are we?" It was Leon.

"We can't be that far from the road," Trudy responded.

"We have to help them." Mark took a step forward and instantly regretted it.

A twig snapping underfoot was all it took for the beast to turn its attention on them.

"Get out of there!" Mark yelled out to Leon and Trudy.

"Yo! Mark! Is that you?"

The creature returned its attention to them. It sensed that its position had been compromised. Letting out a growl that sounded irritated, the creature slithered towards them.

"Run!" they heard Trudy scream.

It was too fast. The monstrous beast charged for them. Leon quickly shoved Trudy out of the way as it slowed its progress.

Flexing his muscles, Leon stared down the creature. "You may be a big boy, but I can handle ya."

Veins building, nostrils flaring, Leon was ready for the fight of his life. In response, the creature showed little sign of interest in a fight. It wanted to consume. That was all.

"Let's go, pretty mouth."

The first strike came but not from the creature. Leon charged the reptilian menace before him. He raised a mighty fist and brought it down hard atop its head. The impact caused it to shake off the numbing wave. Leon recoiled in sheer agony. His fist was reduced to a bloody pulp.

"Goddamnit! So, that's how you want to play?"

Before anyone could say or do anything to stop the madness, Leon mounted the stunned slithering mutation. He wrapped his arms around its girth and held on for dear life. It shook left and right. Then it attempted to buck him off but going up and down. Leon was losing his grip but unwilling to quit.

"Leon!" George's voice could be heard suddenly.

In response, he looked up. "Get out of here!"

The tail rose high in the air, directly above Leon. It was about to lash out when a series of well-placed shots hit it right below the tip. They did not penetrate its scaly hide, they were more like pellets than bullets to the creature. Still, they got its attention momentarily.

"Get off that thing!" Mark cried out.

Leon tightened his grip the best he could. The animal was stronger than he thought. He had wrestled alligators once or twice, but this was something new entirely. Its spiky body was also starting to pierce through his own skin.

It was time to relinquish and run. He threw one more jab, a softer one, into the creature's head and then dismounted it.

"Let's call it a draw," Leon laughed as he ran towards George.

His friend had a look of shock drawn on his face. Leon noticed it right away and turned back. The creature was right behind him.

"Damn you're fast!" That was all Leon had time to say before the jaws engulfed him.

"No!" George cried out.

Lifting Leon into the air, his legs kicking wildly, it bit down once, causing them to snap. One severed immediately, falling with a wet thud in front of George. The other seemed to hold on for dear life, attached by strands of flesh.

Before he could even process what he was seeing fully, Mark grabbed George by the arm and pulled him away. He did not remember much after that moment.

CHAPTER FIFTEEN

It was a sign.

Zoey always hated feeling this way. The idea of guilt racked her mind. This was her fault, and she had no inkling that it was anything but. So much had happened. To boil it all down to her being behind the reunion seemed only fair. Her friends were dying, and it was her who would be to blame whether others thought she should or not. She took one look at George who seemed lost. He and Leon went way back. Their comradery senior year got them into heaps of trouble, but they had a good time every step of the way.

Not only that but Tina and Cecilia were gone. Ripped apart by that damned creature. She was not sure if Mark would ever be the same again. The poor Captain Neil, everyone was dying. She sat under a willow tree in the pitch black. Cradling her legs close to her chest, she began to feel alone despite everyone's closeness.

Fred was pacing back and forth in a fit of rage. The man had lost his own son. Although, painted on his face was a different expression. He carried a sense of vengeance about him that overshadowed his mourning for Joe. A brooding mess, the hunter was a shell of his former self. Even if he would not admit it. His face indicated he had multiple ideas in his mind shooting off like rapid-fire. He wondered what he would tell the boy's mother, how she would cope with it. He needed to figure out how to kill the eeligator.

"We have to get to the high school," Mark spoke up suddenly. "Once it's through with us, it'll have a buffet just waiting for it. We have to warn them."

"Screw that!" George shouted. "We need to get out of here and get some authorities out there to help. It's not our job."

"It may not be our job but it is our duty. Police wouldn't get there in time," Zoey added.

"How nice of you to pick his side. Don't think I don't remember you two," George chuckled.

"This isn't about whose side I'm on," Zoey stated. "It's about morality and right from wrong."
"Can it, you two!" Fred snapped. "That creature is still out there. We don't have much choice in the matter of survival. What we do have is a pistol and a blade. We'll have to make the best of it. I do agree that we should head to the high school."

"Why? There won't be any kind of protection there," George laughed.

"No." Trudy took a step forward from the shadow of a grassy overhang. "No, there isn't but there has to be a computer lab or something to connect us to the outside world. Even a cellphone. I can tap into the computers, and I can contact my boss. Maybe we can get reinforcements out here with the police but, in order for this to reach everyone, it'll have to go viral."

'What the hell are you talking about?" Fred asked.

"People have a right to know."

"You're not a journalist, lady."

"No, but my boss knows someone from the New York Times. Someone high in power," Trudy continued. "Trust me. If I know one thing, your boss is going to try to cover this all up. Do you want your son's death to be swept under the rug like a nudie magazine some kid is trying to hide from his parents?"

The analogy struck a chord with Fred. He knew that it was the exact thing Boudreaux would do to cover himself. There was no doubt he would pay off anyone who was a witness or who lost someone to the creature. He would have already come up with the perfect cover story by now, probably several.

"Alright. We make our way to the high school. Pronto," Fred said.

George shook his head. "This is insane. You saw what it did to Leon. He's bigger than I am and that thing ate him like it was nothing. We don't have a chance."

"We certainly don't by staying here either," Mark said as he stood up.

A faint wind blew through the wisping willows and George felt a sudden chill run down his back. It was a scorching hot summer day and yet he was cold. *Death calling?* he wondered.

"Alright, fearless leader." He turned to Fred and gave a mock salute. "Get us out of here."

***

The event was in full swing. Several people had recognized their fellow classmates right off the bat while it took some time for others to realize. It was not a glorious fashion show or anything, just a group of people in their late twenties hanging out, catching up on old times. Then came the refreshments. Nothing too alcoholic or sweet. It was a very mundane event even with the DJ playing *Bring the Noise* by Public Enemy remixed by Benny Benassi. A few people danced while others just seemed to mingle.

Wendy was becoming increasingly worried about Zoey. She was always one of her favorite students, paying attention and taking everything she said seriously. George Barkley had a tight grip on her back then. She secretly hoped they would break up after high school, but she was not so sure. Her texts were short and to the point. Nothing fancy like years ago. They only seemed to get shorter as the years went on.

"Everything alright?" Bud walked up and placed a tentative hand on her shoulder.

"I still haven't heard from Zoey." Wendy looked out into the night swamp with impatience. She hoped to see the lights from the boat she chartered to illuminate the inky water. They never came. Instead, she heard sloshing sounds, frogs croaking, and crickets endlessly stridulating.

"Can you call her?"

"I tried an hour ago. No response." She shook her head.

"Maybe we should call the police," Bud suggested.

"I would but I don't know if George is with her."

"Barkley? That scum was locked up years ago I thought."

"No. You're thinking of his brother, Scott."

"I guess bad seeds don't grow too far from the tree."

"I guess not."

The sloshing intensified.

"I think there's something out there."

"It's a swamp. I would be surprised if some gators weren't watching us right now."

She shook her head again. "Why was this high school built near a swamp again?"

Bud laughed. "That's just one of the things kids mean when they call it *why man* high school."

They turned back and began to make their way back to the party They did not see the pair of massive red glowing eyes surface and watch them intently. As soon as they were visible, the creature dove again, swallowed into the dark swamp. It was in its element. In the zone. It was reunited back home.

***

"I can't keep going!" George stated, exasperated.

"Maybe if you didn't pound so many beers this wouldn't be happening right now!" Zoey said, out of breath but still eager to move.

"C'mon! Save this argumentative shit for couple's counseling!" Fred shouted. "We're almost there. I can see the glow of the lights off in the distance."

"How much longer?" George begged for an answer.

"Good news is," Fred began, "it looks like there's a clearing over this way. The bad news is that we've still got at least twenty minutes to get there. Especially if we keep this pace."

"Twenty minutes!" George laughed. "You'll be lucky to get me going for twenty more seconds."

"Then stay behind!" It was Zoey who told him what everyone was thinking.

Trudy walked up behind Fred. "We need to keep moving. He's slowing us down. I suggest we have someone stay back with him until he can catch up."

Fred looked around and homed in on Mark. "You, stay with him. The rest of us are going to try and make a break for the school."

"No way!" Mark shouted. "That thing killed Tina and everyone else. I'm going to see this thing through."

The hunter gave him a onceover. Despite his dedication to the chase, he was still in his whites and looked rather pathetic. He was unsure how he had even made it this far. It took determination no doubt but it was still a rather humorous sight. One that he scoffed at.

“Listen, whitey tighty, we don’t have time to waste. You can both catch up later. Right now, we have to make it there. I have a bad feeling it’s already scouring the property while looking for where to strike first.”

“How can you tell?” Zoey asked, fearfully.

“Because it’s how it was trained.”

“How much do you know about its creation?” Trudy wondered.

“Enough. I know that Boudreaux wanted the perfect weapon. Now it’s on a rampage.”

“Boudreaux?” she wondered.

“There’s no time for this!” Fred exclaimed. “We need to get there. The more time we waste with the chitchatting, the higher the body count.”

“Body count?” George raised an eyebrow.

“Yeah! You know. How many people it kills.”

“That’s not what that…” George began.

“Never mind what it means!” Mark cut him off. “Just go! I’ll stay with beer belly!”

Fred wasted no time tearing through the foliage. Trudy followed immediately while Zoey looked back at the two men. They both had an impact on her life. One much better than the other. She could not fathom losing Mark and did not know what life without George would be like. She snapped out of it and hurried after the hunter.

It was a full five minutes before George wanted to move again. In that time, the two had not one word to say to each other. It was a balance between silence and the swamp noise that drove George mad. He could not take this kind of stress. It was a terrible experience for him mentally. Yet he had not one thought of Zoey, how she was doing, her wellbeing.

By the time Mark made his third check around the area, it was certain that the creature was not around. Instead, other monsters waited in the dark. They were close, too close. He turned and saw George trying to get up. He went over to help him but was brushed off.

"I can manage!" he snapped at the near nude man.

"Let's just go. We have a lot of ground to cover," Mark stated.

George sniggered. "Yeah, and a lot of catching up to do too, I presume."

"What are you on about now?"

"I've seen the way you look at my woman."

Mark stood there, flabbergasted. Not only was his patience wearing thin but so was his tolerance for this man. He jabbed a finger into his chest.

"Let's get one thing straight, beer belly. I don't know what you and Zoey do behind closed doors but it's going to end after all this is over."

"The fuck's that supposed to mean?"

"It means, bozo, that if you don't get out of her life, I'll make the call."

"What call?"

"Oh, I'm sure the same one your neighbors have multiple times."

"What neighbors? We're pretty isolated." A thin smile spread across George's lips.

"That explains it all. Nice bit of privacy to beat up your girlfriend."

"You have no proof!"

"News flash, bucko. Her make up's been wearing off this entire time. The bruises have been becoming quite apparent."

"We've been hiking through the swamp for hours. It's going to look like that on her ugly mug."

Mark bit his lip. "Yeah, 'cause trees are notorious for leaving handprints on people's faces."

Before Mark could even turn around, George was on him. He took a few powerful swings, his fists landing in the man's bare back. It was enough to knock both men down. Neither was done though. Before George could get back up, Mark lifted his leg up and sent a kick, full force, into the pudgy man's face. He recoiled but it seemed his body fat just absorbed the impact. Mark went to perform the maneuver again but was grabbed around the ankle.

George gave a mighty tug and pulled Mark closer. He then reached up, grabbed his privates, and pulled. The man let out a shriek and became rigid as his shaft was yanked.

"Okay! Okay!"

"Say you're sorry."

At first, Mark was going to admit defeat. George had him and there was nothing his body could do to retaliate. There was a sickly look on George's face. It was almost ill and morbidly curious at the same time. He reached with his other arm, aiming for Mark's balls. Without even thinking, Mark felt around and snagged a solid object. He wasted no time in bringing it around in a wide arch. The rock smashed into George's temple. A thin stream of blood spilt down the side of his face. His grip weakened as he collapsed, face first, into the dirt below.

He panted with deep sobs in between the breaths. Mark stood up slowly and then sent another swift kick to the side of the man's stomach.

"Bastard!" he spat at him. "I hope you rot!"

Then, in an act that was out of his control, he started to laugh. He bellowed with giggles and shouted up to the heavens. That bastard deserved worse, but this was still a long time coming. Mark turned and sprinted towards the clearing. He just hoped he was not too late.

CHAPTER SIXTEEN

Desire.

Scott Warrington stood before the woman of his dreams. He had thought about her for the last ten years but never mustered the courage to message her on social media. There was never a viable reason to as far as he was concerned. Ten birthdays he could have asked her to partake in, two trips to Europe, an obscene number of art museum visits. They were all decent reasons, but none worked. She was into science fiction and politics. He was at a loss as he was more of a documentary guy and only dabbled a little into the world of politicians, government officials, and the general public.

Then, the unthinkable happened.

A new movie was coming out based on a book from the 1960s. It was titled *Dune*. The gist was that it had a world based around futuristic tech and political science. He read or rather devoured the book in a week and a half. Then he sat down and watched the movie. Afterwards, he waited to see if she had watched it. She was a social butterfly, always posting about what she did and where she went.

Nothing.

No posts about *Dune*. There were other posts around that time though. Things that made his blood boil and jealousy seethe. She met someone. Thankfully for Scott, it only lasted a month. Still, he kept his silence. It was when *Dune Part Two* was released that she posted that she could not wait to go see it. She wanted to desperately see it in IMAX and, even better, she was looking to go with someone. The only hiccup in that plan was that he was at work when she posted her desire. He did not see it until much later and, by then, she was going with a couple of her friends. He did give a silent prayer that they were all women.

Then news of the reunion came up. She was attending and, in turn, he would not miss it. As soon as he spotted her in her floral dress covered in printed red roses, he marched towards her. He was no coward when it came to mingling but, with her, it was going to be a challenge.

She looked at him with interest. "Hey! Scott, right?"

I can't believe it! She remembered my name! "Hey Ashley!"

"How've you been?"

"Oh, you know, same old boring Warrington."

"No! Don't be silly. C'mon! What have you been up to, really?"

Scott gave a shrug. "Not much you could call exciting."

"Try me."

"Well. Hmm. I've visited some art museums this summer, went to Europe a couple of times."

"Ooohhh, fancy." She smiled.

"Yeah." He was not about to focus on his trips. "Oh! I went to the theater for the first time in a long time."

"What'd you go see?"

"I saw the *Dune* movies."

"Really? I thought they were pretty good. Not great like the book."

"I actually thought the opposite. The movies were more engaging than the book for me. I loved both though."

"That's a hot take." She grinned.

"Well, I should probably watch them again to form my final opinion."

"I have them on Blu-Ray! We should do a movie night!"

"Really? You'd be down for that?"

"Sure!" She took a step closer to him. "I think it could be fun."

They were close now.

"Imagine," she began. "The world of *Dune* playing out before us. Trudging through desert, wearing extravagant clothing. Maybe, if we're lucky, I could even ride a sand worm."

He chuckled. "I don't know, I hear they're pretty big."

"Girth's not a problem for me." Her smile melted into his soul.

They continued on like that for minutes, the world around them disappearing into a void. Once the innuendos stopped, they just stared at each other longingly. Desperation to tear each other's clothes off covered their faces. To Scott, he was surprised how forthcoming she had been. She was a woman who knew what she wanted. The only question was when.

"I was hoping you'd grow a pair sooner or later," she told him with a straight face.

"Wanna get out of here?" Scott asked her.

She shook her head. "I think there's plenty of space around here for us."

"You want to do it in a school?" he said a little too loud.

Shushing him with a hand placed gently over his mouth, she then took a couple of steps forward. Scott could smell her freshly cleaned clothes and her skin smelled sweet like an apple. Her dark green eyes stared into his unwavering blue ones.

"I know the perfect spot."

Taking her hand away from his face and grabbing his hand, she guided him towards the school cafeteria. There were unattended tables out there. The hot night air made him sweat a bit. Or he was just nervous. He could not tell which. Maybe both? Regardless, they were now in the middle of the tables. There was one in the middle that she took a seat atop of. She took a sip of her beverage and smiled.

"Alright, tiger. Warm me up."

She opened her legs to him, and he was surprised to see she was not wearing underwear. Her bare privates were exposed to him. He lifted her rose-printed dress and began to caress her legs. His hands went higher and higher as she moaned. Soon, he was rubbing the inside of her thighs. Pushing his glasses up on his face, he went down on her.

"Oh! Oh that's it!"

His tongue prodded around and maneuvered in ways she had yet to experience.

"Oh god! You must've learned a lot in Europe!" she giggled.

Once he stepped back, he began to unzip the fly on his dress pants.

"Fifteen years," he said. "Ever since junior high."

"Come get me, tiger," she demanded.

Quotes from *Dune* began to take over his thoughts. Fear is the mind destroyer, or something like that. He did not want to think about the Sci-Fi epic at the moment. He just wanted Ashley and her rosy, pink parts. Taking a few steps towards her, he lifted his cock and went to insert it. She watched him with bated breath. It was the union they had both been waiting for. For Ashley, it had secretly been even longer than fifteen years.

It would never happen now.

Something long and hard came towards her and it wasn't Scott's manhood. It actually came from above. It looked like a tail but had odd-shaped protrusions sticking out of them, spikes. The appendage slowly lowered itself, now only a few feet from her face.

"What is that?" she wondered.

Scott was looking down at her. He had not seen it just yet. Whatever it was, it did not seem pleasant. Rather, it reminded Ashley of a thorn bush but with scales. The tail then did something unexpected. It swung forward and struck Scott in the eye with one of those spikes.

"Ahhh!" he cried out.

"Scott!" she screamed.

Fear is the mind kil, kil, killer. were his last thoughts as a jolt of electricity shot through his skull. His head ruptured into an explosion of bone fragments and brain matter in seconds.

Ashley watched in shock as the man she was about to give herself to fell to his knees and dropped. His headless body impacted against the table. Blood rocketed out of his stump and shot towards her still open legs. It splattered against her legs and thighs and into her privates. She shut her legs and squirmed.

"Oh god!" she screamed as she got up and off the table.

She did not make it five steps before being scooped up by the predatory creature. It took one chomp to amputate her legs and arms. Her limbless body was then shaken around until it was nothing but a soft, mushy corpse.

***

The clearing was opening even wider as the trio marched through the marshy landscape. Zoey was ready to complain about being covered in filth but stopped herself, realizing there were more pressing matters at hand. She watched as Fred ducked in and out of the shadows, avoiding branches and vines. He was truly in his element. Trudy, on the other hand, seemed ready to break down and cry.

"We're almost there!" Fred exclaimed.

"What are our chances?" Zoey wondered. "If we run into that thing?"

Fred shook his head. "Eeligator is a damn near impenetrable beast. I suggest we get as many people out of there as possible and let the authorities deal with the situation."

"I just wish I could get my cell to work," Trudy said. "I could get a call out to the police."

"Police can't save anyone in this situation," Fred continued. "We're on our own and Wisner and Boudreaux know this. They're counting on us to capture, not kill the experiment."

"How do you plan to do that?" Zoey wondered.

"I'll figure it out when we get there."

The glow from the light set up outside the high school illuminated them more than the moon did now. It was only going to be a few hundred more feet before they were completely away from the swamp and onto the grassy lawn of the property. They all stopped when they heard the screams.

***

Applauding the speech Powers had laid out for them over his retirement, everyone was giddy. Not only would he finally be able to relax and not be so strict, but the parents and children would not have to deal with him anymore. The latter of which no one would dare say. Even the teachers seemed relieved.

Even Wendy and Bud hugged, as did some of the students.

"I know you'll all miss me, terribly so," he said without any humor in his tone. "My replacement has not arrived in Florida yet. She will hopefully carry out the tradition of Wyman High School and make it the best school in the district."

His lack of enthusiasm made it hard to tell if he was being sarcastic or not. While Wyman was not the worst, it certainly wasn't the best.

"I am going to level with all of you," the principal began. "There are many things she and I will go over. Not much will change besides gender."

That time he gave a little chuckle as if to ease the tension he brought about.

Before he could continue, there was shouting coming over from the tree line.

"Everyone needs to evacuate the premises." A grime-covered man with a black beard and tan boonie hat came charging out of the swamp.

The crowd stared at him in surprise. He looked as though he had been through hell and back. His grave expression told them he had seen something horrible out there but there was no indication of what. At least, not yet.

Principal Powers was stationary for a moment. He observed the man with questioning eyes. He had indeed interrupted his speech but, for what purpose, he was unsure. Reluctantly, he decided to go over and see what the problem was. There was no need to send anyone else over. He was in charge of not only the school but the situation. It was all the more a surprise when two women came up from behind him, equally filthy and tired looking.

He recognized one immediately.

"Zoey?" It was Wendy who said her name.

"There's something out there! It's killing people!" she explained while trying not to give too much detail. The more she gave, the more they would undoubtedly laugh.

"What's out there?" a girl in glasses and a smarmy look on her face asked.

"There's no time to explain!" the man stated. "We need to evacuate, pronto!"

Everyone still stood. Some wavered a bit but no one moved.

"What is happening?" Powers asked as he got closer.

"Sir." Fred tried to be polite. "There really is something out there killing people. We need to leave now."

"What? A gator?"

"Something like that."

"Why didn't you call the police?"

"Long story," Trudy added, holding up her cellphone.

"I cannot have you coming here causing a panic. Please get to the high school and call the police." "Trudy," Fred ordered her.

"On it." She marched towards the building. "Where's the entrance?"

"It's past the cafeteria. I'll show you," Wendy said, nervous yet cautious.

Now some people began to move around. One of the younger kids, a girl who wore her black hair in a tight bun, had red rimmed glasses, and had teacher's pet written all over her followed Wendy and Trudy. Bud made his way on stage and towards the podium. He gently grasped the microphone and relaxed himself.

"Everyone. There's no cause for panic. Please follow Mrs. Ronald and remain inside for the time being. I can assure you, everything will be safer in…"

No one saw what did it but he felt it. A bunch of sickly yellow spikes punctured through Bud's chest, skewering and lifting him off the ground for all to see. Blood poured down his chin as one of them had gone through the back of his head and out his mouth. Everyone was stunned at the gruesome sight. The only person to gasp was Powers as he had turned after hearing Bud's speech being prematurely cut off and saw his teacher suspended in the air.

Then came the glow. It started on the ground about twenty feet out. There was a strange *thumping* sound as each foot grew bright. It was heading straight for Bud. Only lasting about ten seconds, the blue light eventually hit the teacher and caused him to spasm and convulse. He could not scream with the spike in his orifice, but he did try. It was a muffled cry of agonizing pain.

A juicy explosion caught everyone off guard as blood sprayed everywhere, splattering all of the students, young and old, and teachers. The wet smacking sound caused Wendy and Trudy to turn back. The student bumped into them just as Wendy let out a horrible scream.

"Geeze, I'm sorry, Mrs. Ronald!'

Wendy paid her no mind and began for the stage. Trudy grabbed her arm and held her back. The student then turned and saw the blood cloud still lingering in the air. It was an odd sight. The crowd was also sprayed with the red substance. It took her a second to process what happened but, by then, it was too late to do anything about it.

CHAPTER SEVENTEEN

Chaos erupted.

A startling sight of macabre mastery, the sight of their teacher being electrocuted to the point of combustion was like a horror movie playing out in front of them. It was made all the worse when the slithering serpent-like specimen made its way around the stage. It kept low to the ground but gave them a devilish grin as it eyed each and every single one of them. Most everyone began to panic but some were so awestruck by the morbid monstrosity that it took them time to process if what they were seeing was real or not. It was unnatural, an unholy abomination.

"What is that thing?" someone screamed from the back of the crowd.

No one answered, no one had an answer. It was there yet it should not have been. The thing that should not be. To most it looked like some weird gator with jagged teeth and only two feet in front. Others got a closer look at its mysterious design patterns. The scales were small but glistened in the Florida moonlight and set up they had. Around its head were spikes of sorts, more so genetic outgrowths of its bulky appearance. By the time the thirty foot menace came into full view, people had just begun to take a step back.

It reared its massive head and watched them. Every single individual who even dared to move, its black slits would narrow onto them. It was as if it were picking who to strike at first. Once everyone began to move, it was game on. It tilted its head back and let out a horrible roar. Behind it, a blue flash illuminated the sky.

A storm was coming. No one had heard of any bad weather on the radar. It was almost as if it came with the creature.

"Run!" was all it took one person to say.

The mass exodus that ensued mostly consisted of self-preservation. Grown men and women pushed past the kids and made for the parking lot on the other side of the school. They had to pass the cafeteria first. Trudy grabbed Wendy and the girl and rushed them inside as the group of scared former classmates barreled past them. They watched as the crazed crowd ran by, only to slip on the ground.

"What the fuck is this?" one of them said as he tried to lift himself off the ground.

"I think it's what's left of Scott and Ashley," another replied, genuinely horrified.

"I think I'm going to be sick," one of the younger adults said as she began to gag.

"Just keep going," the second one replied.

Nine former classmates ran for the safety of the parking lot. Raindrops began to pelt them, but they did not care. Getting a little wet was the least of their concerns, or so they thought.

The creature began towards the fleeing group. On the way, it pushed chairs and some decorative floral set ups out of the way. It knocked into some kids who were hiding under one of the tables. The protrusions on its head caught one of them across the face and slashed his cheek open. The other tried to get up to run but tripped over the mess of scales and barnacles. He found himself rolling down the animal's back. The trip down it ended by him getting poked by one of the scales that punctured through his belly button. The massive animal lifted its tail and shook him off like a flea, sending him flying into another table.

Powers ran towards the two injured boys. Fred and Zoey followed. They got to them and helped them up. Crying, aching with pain, and gushing blood, the classmates were carried over towards the stage, lifted, and placed on the wooden platform. Fred grabbed Zoey and did the same with her. He too then climbed on top.

"What are you doing? We have to help these people!" Powers cried out.

"It's too late. Now, get up here unless you want to end up like your friend."

He was taken aback by the crass comment. The principal did not know what was going on with this creature. It was not until he heard the thumping noise again, and turned and saw the blue light off in the distance did he even begin to piece together the repercussions of being on the wet ground.

"But. But my students." He was a babbling mess.

"C'mon, Principal Powers. You can't do anything if you're dead," Zoey said coldly.

She held out her hand and he reluctantly took it. Both she and Fred helped him on stage.

The Eeligator was able to catch up with the humans, no problem. There seemed to be a different way of handling it though. It was time to put on a show of its full power. It raised its tail and turned it slightly, followed by slamming the spikes into the ground. The charge reached the spikes and the whole ground began to glow blue. Students of old and new who were still in the area were electrocuted in a grisly display of mass execution. All nine older classmates stopped dead in their tracks and began to spasm uncontrollably. They shook and foamed at the mouth. Some students still back at the gathering area also reacted in the same manner. Their bodies were rigid and veins building. Every sensory organ in them was going into overdrive. The pain was unbearable. Some of the attendees' hair caught on fire and, others, their eyeballs popped out their sockets. The whole, excruciating event took ten seconds but, for the victims, it felt like forever. Even if they had no concept of time anymore, they wondered when it would stop, inwardly praying that it would end soon.

It did.

The lawn became a gory geyser of bursting bodies and blood spray. Sixteen people were destroyed, their bodies blown up, flesh and bones scattering everywhere. Death came to all of them so fast that it was almost like a firework, building up then exploding in a dazzling display.

Having a front row seat to the carnage, the two women in the cafeteria were utterly horrified. The girl between them could not help it and screamed. The creature took notice immediately and turned towards the viewing windows that stretched all along the side of the building. It growled and reared back its ugly head. Then, it smashed into the glass, breaking through no problem. Trudy and Wendy went to grab the girl but it was too late.

"Cynthia!" Wendy screamed.

The creature snatched her by her head and dragged her outside. Giving a couple of shakes back and forth, her neck snapped, and head came off the stump. Her lifeless body fell to the ground, blood spilling into a crimson pool around her.

"We have to stop it! It's going to get them!" Powers shouted, angrily.

He went to take a step towards the edge of the stage.

"Don't!" Fred shouted. "You don't know if the ground is electrified!"

The principal turned to him and saw he had a large knife at the ready.

"Give me that!"

"No one handles this baby but me!" He looked to Zoey. "Keep this old fool safe!"

Fred took a few steps past Powers. The ground was not blue anymore. He then looked over his shoulder. "You got this, kid."

Leaping off, he ran for the cafeteria. Zoey thought on what he said as he ran up to the horror that awaited him. As he crossed the lawn, watching out for severed limbs and crimson plasma puddles, he thought back on his wife. She was on the verge of giving up on both he and his late son. Part of the reason Joe was even here was because of her. She had grown distant from both of them. He knew she would not take the news well but there would be that blank stare she'd often have, as if she were looking into some distant void. He then saw the terrible reptilian eel and swore right then and there that, if he could survive this, he would change. If not for his wife, then for himself. In that moment of reflection, he had not realized he already had the blade risen high above his head.

"This is for you, Joe!" he screamed and jammed it down onto the creature's tail, between the spikes.

The Bowie knife broke at the hilt, snapping like a twig. He held back the handle and looked at it in amazement.

"Holy shit!"

The eeligator slowly turned, facing its new challenger. Again, its eyes focused in on the target. It rose back, arching its neck to strike like some abnormal cobra. The action was different, unlike anything Fred had seen up to this point. Then it all made sense. It was not about to strike. It was building something up within. Something so electric, its whole mouth turned blue.

Inaudibly, Fred mumbled something under his breath.

Crack.

It struck, penetrating through its eye. The round had left the barrel and hit its mark. Another one entered the chamber. Fred looked down and saw Mark standing there with Joe's pistol. He had a smirk and wore it like he knew what he was doing. That fact was far from the truth. This was the only chance there was to stop the creature. The great predator seemingly sucked back in the electrical current it was about to expel and faced Mark with its one good eye.

"Run, kid!" Fred screamed.

A raspy roar, one filled with pain and fury, was directed at Mark. He did just as the hunter instructed and ran back into the woods. Branches and thorns cut into him, but he paid no mind. It was deal with that or keep going. If he chose the latter, he would be a dead man for sure. He bent under a low hanging branch and continued to go. A few seconds later, he could hear the beast break through it with ease.

"Shit. Shit. Shit!" he kept repeating.

He began to frantically zigzag around, trying to lose the animal. It was coming for him whether he liked it or not. There was no stopping it. Only run or hide. There was no option for either anymore. Running was just prolonging the inevitable. The creature was too close for him to find cover without it knowing exactly where he was. All he could do was pick up the pace. His bare feet stepped on several rocks and he winced but did not stop. It was coming.

Tackled to the ground suddenly, he felt human hands grabbing a fistful of hair.

"Alright, you bastard!" It was George. "Time for round two."

Mark could only pray the creature would gobble both of them up. Take the asshole with him. He felt George's grip loosen as the noise behind them became too loud for him to ignore. He spun around and faced the beast.

"You want some too?"

He had gone full maniacal. A sense of humor could be heard in his tone. Then, without warning, he dodged the creature's initial strike. It nearly got Mark but George was quick despite his weight and crawled on its back. Instinctively, the eeligator lowered itself to the ground and began to roll around. George held on for dear life. He was being pelted with mud and sticks and felt rocks under him every time he was brought to the ground. They crushed onto his back, causing him to groan in agony. Then, without warning, it stopped. He was underneath it while it lay on its back. Righting itself, George wasted no time in jamming a fist into its empty eye socket.

"How do ya like that?"

It reared its tail and took pleasure in jamming a spike right up his rear. The tail arched at a weird angle before Mark, who had a front row seat to the skewering. Then, he got a crazy idea. With the creature's tail still stuck in George, he got up and slammed into its underside to push it forward. It barely budged but he was slowly making progress. It fought back against his dwindling strength. Any moment it would slam down on Mark, crushing him.

A blue light began to glow on the creature's belly.

"No!" Mark screamed.

If it electrocuted George, his plan would not work. It would all be for nothing.

"Take this, you bastard!"

Mark turned to see Zoey charging them. She climbed up a small rock, mid run, and leapt off. Flying through the air, he watched as she slammed into the tail and the spikes jammed into the creature's skull just as the blue light reached George. It began to shake violently. Electrical waves ran through its body. Mark grabbed Zoey and pulled her away just as the nightmarish monster exploded into a dusty cloud of blood and gore. Chunks of brain matter and skull fragments shot everywhere.

They turned back to see it was over. Finally. It was all over.

The two turned to each other and embraced, then sat back and looked each other over. They looked as though they had been through the jungles of Vietnam during the war and were certainly going to have some memories. There was one big difference though. They had their victory.

CHAPTER EIGHTEEN

Glorious.

The notion that things were getting worse vanished when Zoey and Mark made their way out of the swamp. Trudy and Fred ran up to them and helped them over towards the stage. Wendy was there, sitting on the platform where her beloved Bud once stood. Principal Powers was off to the side, grieving the loss of his students. A few of them had made it to the school building before the electrical blast and, therefore, were unaffected by it. They had their phones out and were calling their parents. In a rare scene of shock and awe, none of them had thought to record the event during the monster's attack.

Fear had driven them to survive instead of gain.

Cruisers eventually arrived as did ambulances and even a firetruck. One of the firefighters gagged as soon as he came around back. The aroma of burnt flesh, hair, and bone was nauseating. It all culminated into a pungent odor that was not meant for those sensitive to smell. It hung in the air, lingering like rotten anal leakage mixed with manure.

Mark was thankful when a blanket was bestowed to him by a paramedic. It gave him the chance to finally cover up. Zoey sat next to him on the edge of the stage, a cool, damp towel pressed against her head. There was a sense of relief to her. Not only was the creature dead, but so was another awful individual in her life. She felt free for the first time in years, a decade to be precise.

"What now?" she asked him.

"I don't know," Mark said weakly. "I feel like a part of me was left back there in the swamp along with Tina."

He was not trying to make a joke. It was not funny to either one of them. He realized his wording and apologized.

"She was a good soul," Zoey said warmly.

"I just don't know how I'm going to cope with it." Tears began to well up in his eyes.

"Whatever happens, we'll get through this together." Zoey placed her hand on his.

He did the same and began to think about the brief time they dated. Going to the fair and him winning her the biggest stuffed animal he had ever seen.

"Why did we stop?" Zoey asked.

"Stop what?"

"Seeing each other?" She tried to make light of the situation.

"George. He tried to pay me to back off but then eventually threatened to get me expelled."

"How could he do that?"

"Well, I sort of cheated on my FCAS test and he knew that."

"I don't think they would've had you expelled for that though. Maybe you'd just have to retake it?"

"Either way, I would've been in trouble." He looked down at himself. "I was young and stupid."

"We all were." She smiled.

He chuckled for the first time in hours. "I guess it takes a mutant monster to show people for what they really are."

"Or bring them together." She inched closer to him and lay her head on his shoulder.

A black van pulled up suddenly. Two men in black tailored suits approached the police and flashed their badges. They were apprehensively allowed to pass. They made a beeline for Fred and Trudy and gently guided them towards the vehicle. Fred shrugged them off at first but, eventually, he eased up. As they passed by, Fred nodded at Mark and Zoey. Both were unsure what to make of the situation.

Soon, they were inside and the van drove by. Inside, Mark and Zoey saw a man with a cold expression looking at them. It was a hauntingly serious look that told them that it was far from over.

Boudreaux sat in the van as they pulled out of the parking lot. He was smoking a cigar and had a glass of brandy in the other. His demeanor changed once they were far enough away from the high school. He was now giggling.

"Quite the show there, huh?"

"What do you want?" Fred asked.

"Patience, my dear fellow. What I want will come soon enough. For now, I think we can agree that my specimen did exactly what it was supposed to do."

"Kill kids?" Trudy said, beaming with fury.

"Kill, yes. However, the kids were just in the wrong place at the wrong time. Do you know how many Iranians would send out their children with a bomb attached to them just to get a point across."

"Then what's your point?" Fred asked.

"I don't want to send more innocent off to fight. I'd much rather have monsters roaming the villages and towns of the enemy."

"You couldn't even control this one, had to send me and my now dead son off to do your dirty work!" Fred looked like he wanted to lunge at the man.

"If you had completed your job and reached the destination, we could have."

"Oh yeah?" Fred scoffed.

"Implants, they would have trackers and shock collars implemented in them. They were all waiting back at base for the delivery that never showed."

"Enough of this!" Trudy shouted. "What is it that you want?"

The businessman smiled; his leather jacket stretched as he leaned forward towards them. His voice low and raspy, he began to speak. "I want to know everything that happened."

"You have cameras out there. You should already know," Fred stated.

"Not everywhere. I want firsthand encounters. How the creature acted, reacted, and fought back."

"It didn't fight back. It just killed. It was downright indestructible," Fred explained.

"Yet it was destroyed."

"By sheer fucking luck and ingenuity."

"We'll have to work on that." Boudreaux pondered for a brief moment. "Anything else?"

"It's smart. It went after someone when there was a fresh body to be taken."

"Why didn't it take the latter?"

"Because he was already stuck in some vines."

"That's wonderful!" Boudreaux smiled.

"You're a sick bastard!" Trudy added.

"Oh, my dear." He grinned. "You have no idea. What is to come next will make you rethink modern warfare and maybe, just maybe, you'll see where I'm coming from."

"Fat chance!"

"Just you wait and see." Boudreaux leaned back and took a sip from his glass and then exhaled. "Ah. Just you wait and see."

The End

SEVEREDPRESS

@severedpress
/severedpress

Check out other great

Sea Monster Novels!

Michael Cole

CREATURE OF LAKE SHADOW

It was supposed to be a simple bank robbery. Quick. Clean. Efficient. It was none of those. With police searching for them across the state, a band of criminals hide out in a desolate cabin on the frozen shore of Lake Shadow. Isolated, shrouded in thick forest, and haunted by a mysterious history, they thought it was the perfect place to hide. Tensions mount as they hear strange noises outside. Slain animals are found in the snow. Before long, they realize something is watching them. Something hungry, violent, and not of this world. In their attempt to escape, they found the Creature of Lake Shadow.

C.J. Waller

PREDATOR X

When deep level oil fracking uncovers a vast subterranean sea, a crack team of cavers and scientists are sent down to investigate. Upon their arrival, they disappear without a trace. A second team, including sedimentologist Dr Megan Stoker, are ordered to seek out Alpha Team and report back their findings. But Alpha team are nowhere to be found – instead, they are faced with something unexpected in the depths. Something ancient. Something huge. Something dangerous. Predator X

SEVEREDPRESS

@severedpress
/severedpress

Check out other great

Sea Monster Novels!

Michael Cole

MEGALODON VS COLOSSAL SNAKE

Brought to life by the miracle of DNA cloning, a 93-foot Megalodon shark has escaped captivity. With an insatiable appetite and unmatched aggression, it travels west for the Georgia coast, leaving a path of destruction in its wake. Bullets and harpoons can't penetrate it, steel nets can't hold it, and it's only a matter of time before the whole world finds out about it. In a race to stop the beast, the organization responsible recruit a marine biologist and a herpetologist to develop a plan to catch it. To do it, they must unleash the company's other genetically modified experiment—a 150-foot snake, resurrected from the DNA of the mighty Titanoboa. The pursuit leads to inevitable combat, and the scientists are forced to witness the deadly realities of genetic tampering. As the battle escalates, it is clear nobody is safe...and that nature never intended for these beasts to return. As the destruction mounts, and the death toll climbs, the true loser of Megalodon vs. Colossal Snake is humanity.

Tim Waggoner

TEETH OF THE SEA

They glide through dark waters, sleek and silent as death itself. Ancient predators with only two desires – to feed and reproduce. They've traveled to the resort island of Las Dagas to do both, and the guests make tempting meals. The humans are on land, though, out of reach. But the resort's main feature is an intricate canal system . . . . . . and it's starting to rain.

Printed in Dunstable, United Kingdom

72479818R00094